TIMESLIP

TIMESLIP

N.M. Kirby

Matador
9 Priory Business Park,
Wistow Road, Kibworth Beauchamp,
Leicestershire. LE8 0RX
Tel: (+44) 116 279 2299
Fax: (+44) 116 279 2277
Email: books@troubador.co.uk
Web: www.troubador.co.uk/matador

ISBN 9781783061440

British Library Cataloguing in Publication Data.
A catalogue record for this book is available from the British Library.

Typeset by Troubador Publishing Ltd, Leicester, UK

Matador is an imprint of Troubador Publishing Ltd

Printed and bound in the UK by TJ International, Padstow, Cornwall

To Richard, Jack and Rob
and to all family and friends for their enthusiasm
and encouragement throughout

CHAPTER ONE

They ran through the corridors of the large, familiar building and were anxious to find some normality. They stopped abruptly and Jude leaned sideward in order to peer through the small glass panel in the centre of the door. He had been looking forward to this moment and yet now that he was standing here he was dreading it for fear of their reaction. They were all in there, just as they had been earlier. His eyes scanned the room until they fixed upon Davy, the lecturer, who was standing at the front. He had put his pen down and held on to it, as though momentarily lost in thought, but then turned, pushed his shoulders back and pointed to the screen. Susanna began to lean across Jude, trying to get a glimpse of the scene. Her breathing had become erratic. 'You okay?' Jude asked quietly, sensing her apprehension. She nodded and without further hesitation they barged in.

Davy had begun talking about the social history of the nineteenth century. His class was avidly watching him; he always brought the subject to life, describing vivid moments with interesting anecdotes. Before the break he had been talking and showing portraits for nearly an hour and soon the students would have a chance to have their say when they discussed the topic openly. Yet he was stalling as two of his students had failed to return and he sensed something was wrong. He rolled the pen around the palm of his hand. He knew they were keen on this particular part of history, so why had they not come back from the mid-morning break, which was usually enough time just to grab a drink? His mind kept drifting. They were in their second year of the history course.

He had watched them become acquainted for the first time two years ago, and their friendship was strong and had taken off right from the start. Together, he thought, they made great companions.

Davy placed the pen on the desk and stared down at it. He turned to the screen and was just about to speak when they suddenly burst through the door looking wretched and they were dressed differently. Susanna had a crumpled deep blue flared dress on and was carrying a cape and shawl, and Jude was wearing an unusual coat with a brightly patterned waistcoat underneath and was carrying a hat. They certainly weren't wearing those clothes earlier, he thought, and tried to recall if the Drama department were putting on a production this week. The whole class stared at them; they were out of breath and desperate to speak.

'Listen!' said Jude, 'you'll never believe it – we intended to come straight back, but we just got drawn in.' Susanna, known to the class as Susie, was standing next to him looking tearful, yet smiling. Davy sat down with the rest of the class and stared in bewilderment at Jude, whose normally straight, black hair was dishevelled and wiry and his pale green eyes were shining excitedly. Susie stood wavering next to him, her ash blonde hair was wild and stiff with pieces of hedgerow strewn through and there were scratches all over her face. There were whispers around the room and as the noise grew, Susie became emotional and agitated as she tried to get the attention of the class. She slammed her hand down on the table.

'Listen to Jude, listen to what he's got to say; we've gone back in time. We've seen London as it used to be!' Jude touched her shoulder, gently calming her, and they both sat down. Although he was only twenty, Jude had from a young age been interested in the dimensions of time. He firmly believed that consciousness always moved along with time and that time lived freely by the conscience is very different from time which is certified by the clock and calendar. He didn't really know what had happened back there but he felt that he finally had proof and Susanna was here to verify it. Surely they will get it? Anyway, he thought, here goes.

'We slipped through the hedge at the back of that field,' he said pointing over towards the window, 'we were on our way to the canteen, but then Susie saw the horses.'

'They hardly ever come to the edge of the field, they are always in the next one,' interrupted Susie, 'so I just wanted to see if they would respond and come over to us.'

Jude carried on, 'we didn't have any bags with us as it was just a coffee break – I knew I had a pound in my pocket, enough for two drinks. But as we neared the hedge we both felt a sudden pull, the horses disappeared and we were left with a sensation as though we were rolling around in the air at speed, and then everything went blank and we were left feeling unpleasantly disoriented. When it stopped we both sat still for ages, trying to work out what had happened. We realised that just as we were reaching for the horses, some kind of whirlwind had pulled us quickly through the hedge. We found ourselves in a dry, dusty street.' A couple of students muffled their laughter. Ignoring them he glanced round the room. Davy and everyone else in the room were staring and listening intently, transfixed.

'The sun was shining hazily,' he continued, 'we sat dazed for a while on the dusty edge of the road sensing the atmosphere was all wrong. It felt warmer for a start, we had left a grey, drizzly day and now the sun was peeping through. Suddenly without warning a horse and carriage whipped past ripping off a large piece of Susie's skirt and leaving it trailing behind. We jumped up quickly, stared at each other in disbelief and tried to gather our thoughts. Susie began yelling and asking what had happened over and over while I just sat in a daze saying that I wasn't sure, it was as though we had stepped into a different world. After going over the possibilities, we dusted ourselves down and cautiously started walking down the road in silence, as if in a dream until Susie stopped suddenly, refusing to go any further, repeating that we didn't know where we were or what was out there. I agreed, but suggested we went just a bit further to see what was around the corner; after all I was scared too. But before I knew it Susie was marching back towards the place that we fell through, convinced that there must be part of a hedge that had caved in, leaving a wide gap.' Jude glanced briefly at Susie as if to gain her assurance.

'So, without further hesitation we retraced our steps, stopping at the point where we guessed we had entered, but there was nothing unusual about the hedge. We both began furiously bending the branches, waiting for that force of energy that had swept us off our feet only moments ago. It was hopeless and I could see Susie was rapidly beginning to lose it, but I tried to stay calm. I asked her where she thought the piece of skirt went. She tried to focus and we went back and forth, scanning the ground but could only see fallen leaves. Susie quickly became agitated and was soon in tears. I felt awful – and seeing her like that made me feel responsible somehow, so I wandered up and down once more until it became obvious we were getting nowhere. Not knowing what else to do we followed the direction of the carriage, hoping that someone somewhere could shed light on it all…'

Susie glanced over at the class and then at Davy. All was quiet with an air of expectancy. She wasn't sure why Jude had paused, but she could see he was becoming emotional. She had become accustomed to his sentiment and suddenly felt very protective towards him. She gently encouraged him, 'Go on, tell them the rest.'

Jude checked out the scene behind him. Just off the road to the left he could hear the gentle creak of sails moving slowly round. He made a mental note of the windmill as a landmark. As they began walking they noticed how completely different the scenery was; the college campus had disappeared and instead they were in the countryside. After a mile or two of country lanes they came across three houses in a row and stopped at the first house. Jude crouched down to see what kinds of people were living there but Susie remained standing behind him. A young woman was attending a vegetable patch in the front garden. She was wearing a long, heavy looking skirt with a sash made of silk around her waist and a beige shawl. She had her hair partly gripped, was wearing a lace flat cap, but wasn't wearing any shoes.

Susie stood calmly watching and then decided to approach her and was the first to speak.

'Good morning, we were just passing by and–' The girl stood up straight, looking them up and down – she thought they appeared a little disagreeable and somewhat dazed, but having a generous nature decided to overlook it.

'Well, I get lots passing by here. I suppose you're hungry after walking all that while?' she said, interrupting. Her eyes settled on Jude.

'I don't mind, travellers from the country pass by here all the time, this little house being on the edge of town and nothing for miles in the direction you came.' She looked them up and down again swiftly, 'your clothes are a bit strange.'

Susie tried to think quickly on her feet, 'we just wear the rags we're given, we'll get new clothing soon,' and touching her hair added quickly 'I lost my ribbon,' and glanced at Jude. The girl appeared baffled, but shrugged and said, 'I was just about to go out but if you go into the yard, I'll fetch you something to eat.'

'Oh, great,' replied Susie, trying not to sound too desperate, she felt really hungry after all. Jude looked uncomfortable and hesitant, so she steered him round the side of the house and into the yard and told him he had better speak up soon.

Susie and Jude had an affable friendship. They were relaxed around each other and there was often no need for subtlety. They were both at college and this year had been learning about the social aspects of Victorian cities. Jude wondered whether it was possible that they had stumbled directly into that era and were on the outskirts of London. He had become nervous and suspicious and decided to take one moment at a time. Looking around the back yard they saw piles of general brick-a-brack and upturned boxes and bits of wood. A mass of trailing blackberries were growing against the back wall. The sun felt warm on Susie's back and she found herself instantly lowering her guard, unlike Jude, who was frowning and whispering, 'what do you think she'll bring out?' He couldn't believe that he was even here. He had held it together when he saw Susie unravelling at the edges, yet now she was acting as if all this was normal. He felt really out of place and told her that they must go straight back, but before she could reply the young woman returned with some bread and butter.

Her name was Eva, she said, and handed them chipped white earthenware plates and told them to take the food and eat. She regarded them closely as they winced a little at the specs of dirt on the plates, but they took the food gratefully and ate quickly; after all it was almost lunchtime when they fell through the hedge and who knew when they might eat next; they should have been in the canteen by now.

They sat in a stunned, awkward silence, desperately

thinking what to say when Eva asked who they were. Afraid of being totally honest, Susie told her that they were cousins who had walked from the outskirts of London and were looking to make their fortune in the city. Jude admired her inventiveness and they sat in a trance watching Eva chew, waiting for her reaction.

'Like just about everybody else,' replied Eva eventually. Jude and Susie exchanged relieved glances that their story was believed and that they were right about their whereabouts. Feeling more confident Jude began to ask a couple of questions in return.

'Do you live here alone?'

'Yes,' replied Eva, 'but my neighbours drop in all the time.'

'Oh – and do you work?' he asked. She hesitated at this.

'I make straw-plaits for a hat shop. It's good money. I'm not going there today, though.'

'Why not?' asked Jude, innocently.

'It's Sunday, of course!' replied Eva, clearly surprised that he had to ask and added, 'I'm going to the markets near the river now. It gets very busy at first, but quietens down in time for the services. I suggest you come with me, there's nothing for you around here, I'll show you the way to the riverside.' Jude and Susie both looked at each other and shrugged. Eva was putting on some black lace-up boots, which Susie noticed weren't dissimilar to her own. As she straightened up she looked curiously at Susie.

'Look at that tear; what are you wearing anyway, that's a funny lookin' dress, and where are your petticoats?' she said, quite astonished. Jude cringed and waited for Susie's reply. He could tell she was nervous by the way she was clenching her hands.

'I discarded them as we were walking, they were too heavy,' she said, and added quickly, 'is there anywhere I can find a second-hand dress? We have very little money left.' Eva began to reply that there was the Rag Fair, then shot a glance at Susie's silver charm bracelet, 'I'll give you a few shillings for one of those ornaments that dangle from your wrist.' Susie automatically covered the bracelet with her other hand; she paused for a moment and looked over at Jude, who nodded.

'Well, okay,' she said, slowly removing a small silver heart. If they were to go any further they would certainly need the money, but she was worried; she had no idea where she was and now she only had four charms left.

CHAPTER TWO

Eva, Susie and Jude began wandering through the streets towards the river. As they walked, Jude noticed the streets were getting busier, but many houses, shops and gardens were unfinished. It felt as though construction had begun everywhere and was then abandoned. As the streets became more populated he became acutely aware of a terrible stench from a combination of animal manure and rotten food. It ripped through his throat making him feel nauseous and he glanced over at Susie who looked rather pale and like she was trying not to breathe in at all. She had honed in on the smokiness in the air that appeared to encompass everything; it was an assault on her senses and she was desperately trying to avoid openly choking. They had walked a couple of miles to reach the market which wasn't quite as far as the river and as they approached the market traders Eva surprised them by pointing and saying, 'well that's it, I'm going this way, get your clothes from over there; if you want to venture further into the city just walk towards the blue dome of St. Pauls.'

They started to thank her but she seemed quite eager to disassociate herself from them, quickly disappearing into the crowds. They looked round; well at least this established that they were in London and then they looked at each other; they did look glaringly different. They guessed it must be the absence of hats that made passers-by stare and sneer. They were feeling decidedly uncomfortable and intimidated now that they were on their own; the only consolation being that they felt relieved that they didn't have to hide their culture shock from Eva any more. Now they could openly gasp at the concoction of smells, sights and sounds that were hitting their senses. The noise was astounding; animals' hooves clattering on the cobbles, grunting pigs, and the screeching of costermongers' barrows as they were loaded with meat, fish and vegetables and worst of all men and women yelling at the tops of their voices trying to sell their wares.

They realised they couldn't walk around much longer looking the way they did and went in the direction of the Rag Fair that Eva had mentioned to them. They needed clothes that would help them to blend into society better. Susie turned to Jude.

'If it's the market on Rosemary Lane, I think it's famous for being unregulated, maybe the clothes are stolen, but I don't suppose it matters – second-hand, third-hand – we just need to buy anything. You need a cap or hat and maybe waistcoat and jacket, I think you're alright in those corduroys and I need to get out of this skirt and find something to tie my hair up with.' Jude acknowledged her without smiling. He was quite surprised at how she was taking the upper hand. At home she had just been good fun to hang around with, even though they were often in larger groups. But this was different, the situation was tense and maybe this was her way of coping; he'd let her get away with it – for now.

The Rag Fair was a huge menagerie of street stalls selling a mixture of old clothes and boots and was unbelievably busy. People jostled and manoeuvred in and around the stalls as if in a perpetual hurry. Clothes were piled high on the floor near the tables and it was difficult not to be tripped up by the sheer volume of cloth. There was a melancholic atmosphere, as if a shadow had been cast over the whole market. Someone barged into Jude without looking, and stumbled past without as much as a glance. Then they found a large stall tumbling over with colourful, quality clothes. Susie bought a deep blue dress and petticoats, white blouse to go underneath, short cape and bonnet for herself and a brown velvet crop jacket, waistcoat and top hat for Jude, who kept his own white shirt on, but folded the collar inwards and upwards to look less conspicuous. Surprisingly the whole lot only amounted to very little, so Susie paid a few pence more for a silk handkerchief which she tied round his collar in the shape of a loose bow tie. She had seen a couple of well-dressed gentlemen in the crowds and thought it prudent that Jude appeared more like them. They fled down a side alley, littered with broken wicker baskets and discarded old food and quickly changed, leaving their unwanted clothes in a heap by an old wooden bin.

Susie stopped suddenly.

'Let's think a minute. We don't want to get lost. And what about getting back? I'm worried now, we need to remember which way we came – and we've only got a small amount of money and what do we do tonight?' She was clearly panic-stricken. 'Look, would you just stop? You're speeding around at ninety miles an hour,' snapped Jude. Susie glared at him.

'Well, no thanks to you, we might be stuck here,' was her retort.

'What do you mean?'

'Well, if you hadn't have wandered off as soon as we arrived, we might not even be here.' Jude was confused; he wasn't expecting such an outburst.

'If you remember, we both walked off together, I don't remember going first.'

'Well, you did.' Susie turned away from him; she wasn't sure whether she was angry, afraid, excited or what.

They were silent. Jude stood still for a moment thinking fervently and then he said more calmly.

'Don't worry – I've been trying to keep a mental note of the way we came. As for money, we know people will take silver, you've got a few charms left and I've got a watch and a pound coin in my pocket; we've seen two gold smelters already.'

She turned to face him.

'But they won't recognise the coin; it'll cause too much curiosity, drawing attention to us.' She spoke quickly but quietly, 'whatever we do we must try and get to grips with all the coins they use. Forgery and coining are some of the biggest crimes here; the punishment is tough and I don't want to stay around for that.'

'Okay, okay,' replied Jude, who had raised his voice. He was trying not to panic about the impact of his obvious ignorance. People had begun looking their way. He decided to quash the tension; he had to make sure they didn't draw any more attention to themselves. He clasped her hands in his as if to make a pact.

'I suggest we try and keep out of everyone's way and as soon as it gets dark find somewhere and stay there. Then tomorrow we go back.' Susie nodded eagerly; the last thing she wanted was confrontation. She was glad to have a plan and decided to put aside natural concerns of how they would return to their future and all that was familiar.

Looking at their surroundings, they couldn't deny they were both fond of this era and knew it quite well. They also loved London and had recently been on two college excursions; but this was something else. It felt like a small town rather than a city, and the skyline was low, only towers and steeples could be seen. It was much more overcrowded though; it made modern Oxford Street seem like a quiet village and they were well aware of all the downfalls; the dangers of petty theft, poor hygiene and adulterated food.

On the outskirts of the markets the road surfaces were quite rough with loose cobblestones that made it awkward to walk on, some almost the size of small boulders. Around here there were more street sellers, the men were wearing silk waistcoats in vivid colours and patterns and the women were wearing broad hats; it was as though this entitled them to sell aggressively, but these stalls eventually thinned and as they headed out towards the main thoroughfare they began to see various taverns, which at last were a more comforting sight.

They passed long rows of tall, terraced houses, which looked new and there were a few more congenial street sellers here, but the whole area in general had quietened slightly. There was a strong smell of fish, reminiscent of the market, and nearby a man was selling mackerel, with a crowd gathered around eating it. The smell was so strong that Susie almost retched and they hurried past. Farther on they passed several oyster stalls, some of which were so basic they resembled ironing boards. Another was more substantial with three men standing around wearing either bowler hats or caps and a sign hung above the large table of shells saying '*Best Cleethorpes Oysters*' five for 6d and Jude was tempted, but thought better of it. Looking around he felt that he had walked straight on to the set of an old western, with the assortment of waistcoats, jackets and kerchiefs that the men were wearing.

They carried on walking, realising that the streets were getting quieter the further towards lunchtime it got. It allowed them to properly take in their surroundings. It was amazing to see such low structures; the only thing that stood out was the distant spires, the tallest points for miles. They could hear the chimes of church bells and Susie imagined the atmosphere was like it always used to be on a Sunday, according to her mother; all the shops closed and the streets quite dead, only to ripple slowly back to life in the early evening with the opening of the pubs.

They could still see one busy street and curiosity led them down it. There were rows of men with bird cages, bird fanciers most likely, who seemed to be involved in some kind of trade, although it was exchange rather than buying and selling. They were all chatting animatedly, trying to get the best swaps and there was obviously a big demand for them as cages were spilling out from the pavements on to the roads. Some birds had got loose and were hopping about but not trying to fly away. A few other smaller animals were there, the most unusual being hedgehogs. Jude and Susie kept their distance and tried not to get involved in any exchange, eventually walking on the other side of the street. They had already seen a monkey on a lead, walking next to its owner and the place was beginning to feel like a zoo. As they approached the other end of the street they could see a park.

As they sauntered through they could hear an orchestra playing in the central bandstand. There was quite a gathering sitting and watching, so they remained at the back and sat on the ground. The musicians were in uniform and sounded very good. Whilst they listened Susie collected her thoughts. She tried to understand why she wasn't feeling hysterical and the only reason she could think of was that her survival instincts had taken over; she knew they could not afford to be discovered at all costs. Jude was enjoying the novelty of being anonymous. He wondered what they would all be doing back at home now and whether they realised he was even missing yet. The last tune subsided and the musicians began to pack their instruments away. Jude and Susie felt rooted to the spot; they had no idea where to go next. Eventually they stood up having seen chandelier lights appearing in the centre of some of the establishments and back on the street could hear the accompanying clatter of plates and glasses being stacked. They edged closer to one of the doors to look at a notice which read *'closed between 3-5 o'clock Sundays'* and guessed that this must be one of those jazzy gin palaces, a brighter alternative to the pub.

The sun was starting to go down and seeing that places were beginning to open up again made them excited and uncertain at the same time. They used the lit up cafes and restaurants as a guide to take them towards the town. The smell of manure was still quite strong, but there was always a young man around swiftly scooping piles of it up. In the distance they could hear the faint bleating of animals; it felt quite rural, yet within minutes they passed all types of shop fronts, some with goods under canopies, diners and chophouses and they stopped where a small crowd had gathered. A man was standing next to a cart, pulled by a donkey and yelling 'plum duffs, get 'em here, halfpence each'; they looked like sweet puddings boiled in cotton bags and were obviously popular so they bought one each, but nothing more. Nerves had prevented real hunger, and the thought of what extra delights might be found in the food, like builders plaster, was really off-putting.

A group of men seemed to be staring at the way they were eating and Jude began to feel threatened, especially when he noticed one of them split his pie with a knife and then rip it open and press it into his mouth. Feeling uneasy he muttered to Susie 'we'd better not stay here long, let's move on quickly.' People were either chatting in the street, or sitting in groups around piles of rubbish. They saw a sign for a Temperance Tavern which was being monitored outside by a woman pouring out lemonade to swaying passers-by and then towards the end of the same road they stumbled across a coffee station and decided this would be a better place to stop. It had an eclectic mix of people sitting and standing around it – women, young and old, wearing bonnets or lace caps, an elderly man in a suit and long jacket, and a man in uniform. Amazingly everyone was drinking out of china cups and saucers; it was like an oasis of respectability amongst very crude surroundings. Jude wanted to clear something up.

'I don't know about you, but I was afraid at first. I didn't know what to expect, what we might have to face – but all this seems in a strange way familiar to me.' Susie appreciated his candour.

'Well, if you want to know I do somehow feel compelled

to venture further, I like the fact that it's all going on in the street – but it's a risk – let's just make sure we stick together.'

They heard some music start up. It sounded like a piano organ and a few people around it began to shuffle their feet, a couple of women started dancing. Then more people joined in. There was such spontaneity about it, it took Susie by surprise. Another man joined the group playing a clarinet softly and so they hung around for an hour or so, perched on two barrels, soaking up the sociable atmosphere, but they were both feeling tired and emotional and what they really needed to do now was to find somewhere to stay for the night.

As they walked along late afternoon turned into early evening. They watched lamplighters light the gas lamps individually, climbing ladders to reach the higher ones and before long there was pitch blackness everywhere; it was very strange seeing London lit only by odd gas lamps here and there. It was still quite lively, but it was as though everyone was groping around in the dark. The sounds in the street had become a series of echoes and muffled speech and they immediately began to feel vulnerable. They avoided small alleyways, instead staying within the wide passages. Although they were now anxious to find somewhere to stop they didn't want to venture into filthy buildings and stay amongst vagrants. They had thought of a room shared with others in a cheap lodging house but instead quickly decided to look for an inexpensive unfurnished room and as they had seen a small shop with a sign designating it as a Holborn confectioner, they decided that Holborn was as good an area as any.

Walking through the rambling streets Susie saw a man who looked Italian playing a harp. It was such a remarkable, tranquil scene that they stopped and listened for a while. As he was standing outside a row of houses, some of the occupants came out and stood and listened too. The harpist wasn't pushy at all; every now and then he took his hat off and held it out to passers-by hoping for some money. Jude noticed a small girl standing nearby selling muffins. She was carrying a huge wicker basket and had about eight left. He decided to buy a couple but was curious about her.

'It's a bit late to be selling still, isn't it?'

'I have to sell 'em all before I can go home, sir,' she replied.

Jude thought that was awful and said without hesitation, 'I'll buy the rest.'

'Thank you, goodnight, sir,' and she ran off in haste.

'What was that? Did I hear you buy all the muffins?' asked Susie.

'I just felt really sorry for her; she only wanted a couple of pennies.' Susie didn't reply but felt equally sad; the whole idea of children working like this was appalling.

They moved on and after dismissing some of the tumble-down rotten black brick buildings they came across a house that looked neater and cleaner, at least from the outside. They went into the doorway and asked the round, severe looking woman about lodging there. 'It'll cost you 1s 4d for the week,' she said without any pleasantness and proceeded to show them the room. It was totally sparse, with not even a mattress, but by now they were just relieved to find a space of their own to hide away and have time to think. They nodded to show their approval and Jude handed over some of his money straight away to secure the place. So far the shillings they had been given had lasted them well, but Jude could see they needed to be careful now. Susie was busily looking around.

'There's nothing to sleep on, but at least there are no pests,' she said scanning all corners of the room. Jude didn't say anything; he was weary; he had already noticed plenty of rats around outside, scuttling between floorboards and in and out of every conceivable gap, even in broad daylight, but perhaps Susie hadn't noticed them yet.

'I don't care; my feet are aching,' she continued, taking her boots off and rubbing her toes, 'I'm happy sleeping on the floor – I'll just roll some of my petticoats up for a pillow,' and she began fussing around, using clothing as a pretend mattress.

'You can have some as well if you want,' she said suddenly seeing him looking pensive. She stopped what she was doing and looked purposefully at him, 'what are we playing at – we're acting as if this is all normal.'

'It is normal, for now–' he replied.

'What would happen to us if we could never get back?' Jude had thought of nothing but this.

'I still don't see why we shouldn't. If there's a way in, there's a way out. We just need to make sure we remember which hedge we came through, I calculated about three miles into the countryside. I think when we retraced our steps we were quite a bit out.' He was trying to arrange his corner of the room. 'Don't you want to stay as long as we can? Or do you just want to go home tomorrow?' Hearing his confidence made her pause and consider it but she still wasn't sure. She went over to her makeshift bed and sat on it.

'When do you suggest we go back?'

'When the money's run out I guess,' said Jude, whose voice trailed off uncertainly.

'Let's decide in the morning shall we?' she said conclusively, yawning and stretching her legs out.

Jude sat down next to her and stroked the side of her hair. 'Don't worry. You're just tired. Hey, remember when we missed the last train from Paddington a couple of years ago and the next train was at six o'clock in the morning, we practically camped out like this. I wonder if the station's changed much,' he said, wistfully, but she had already gone to sleep.

CHAPTER THREE

They awoke to the deafening sound of general street noise which made them jump up and run to the small window. Outside there were already hordes of people coming and going, some stopping and sitting, but the main flow appeared to be going towards the heart of the city, the workers in their thousands. It felt surprisingly warm and was a relief after a constant breeze through the window in the night had left them cold. Jude could see Susie was really excited and guessed she had no intention of going back, so he said nothing more about it; he couldn't resist the urge to find out more and more either, he knew it was too good an opportunity to miss.

'Shall we just make our way towards the shops in the main thoroughfares, I want to see what they're selling,' she said. Jude was delighted she wanted to keep going and was amused at her keenness to go shopping. Susie was aware that this wouldn't have been Jude's first choice, but was really keen to explore the retail side of things, in particular to see what kind of clothes were being sold. She shook out the petticoats and put them back on and they both pulled on their boots; Jude was much quicker so he ran over to help Susie lace hers, and they eagerly made their way outside. They turned left and began walking with the crowds. They noticed there were a few pigs mingling in amongst them. Here we go again, thought Jude, flinching and taking in a sharp breath.

It was around seven-thirty in the morning. Jude still had his watch with him, but kept it hidden in case it caused too much curiosity. It was obvious people here began the day very early. The dusty streets were dampened down with water by street sweepers, yet rubbish had been thrown into open drains. Errand boys could be seen running to hold horses for drivers who temporarily stopped their carriages. As they walked further along they noticed all the cracks in the road surfaces, but the aromas became intermittently more pleasant. Immediately they were hit with the smell of fried bacon, warm bread and coffee. They wandered around a maze of passageways, noticing early breakfast houses bustling with workers and lots of separate stalls which looked just like kitchen tables set up as eating stations. 'Let's stop here shall we?' said Jude. He was starting to feel peckish and noticed this particular stall was selling saveloys. 'I'll have one of those,' he said to the stallholder, 'and I'll just have a boiled egg please,' said Susie. They purchased these and two cups of coffee. 'Not quite like a latte is it?' said Susie grimacing and vowed to spend a bit more on coffee the next time as this tasted a bit like chicory with some unrecognisable flavour added, could it be fig?

They sat for a while, contemplating the scene. Everything was so vibrant. The roads were thick with people, carts, horses and dogs. Susie watched as children ran around barefoot, grabbing food and quickly disappearing. She could see why they were sometimes referred to as street squirrels and thought that no one here could possibly feel lonely amongst these crowds, despite having a fundamental solitary existence. Perhaps it was the poor people that gave a melancholy, yet edgy vibe to the street scene. Nearby a boy was selling matches and newspapers, which gave Jude an idea; he pulled Susie back with a start.

'Just a minute – stay here.' He edged along to the side of a stall and stood close to a man holding a stack of broadsheets and managed to glance at the date written at the top. He froze at the realisation of what he had read, '*Monday 1st September 1851.*' He looked around him again. Can this be real? He was rubbing his face, deep in thought, and then looked at Susie who was standing cautiously still, watching him.

'What is it? Is it what I think it is – how far back in time have we gone?' she asked, looking up and down at the packed streets buzzing with activity.

'It's 1851!' he replied.

'My God, I guessed it was Victorian London but I didn't realise we had gone back this early. Do you realise we can experience everything we've ever learned first-hand. We can even visit The Great Exhibition!' said Susie, thrilled, although Jude being more cautious tried to contain his emotion.

They strolled further, finding themselves wandering through Cheapside and took in all that the market stalls and small shops were displaying. Presently they turned into Cornhill. Jude saw a sign saying *Jerusalem Coffee House*. They walked to the entrance and he gingerly poked his head round the door. 'It looks cheery in here, hub of the news by the looks of it. Come on,' he said touching Susie's shoulder, guiding her through the narrow door.

It made a change from buying refreshments on a street corner. The place was fairly large and consisted of various city news rooms. People in uniform dominated the scene, possibly merchants and captains, and although the atmosphere was relaxed, there was a real buzz about the place. Before they ordered a drink they wandered through to The Subscription Room. Here there were rows and rows of files of books about East India Shipping. 'Look at all these,' said Jude in awe. The books were there for everyone's use. Nearby was a well-dressed man in a grey jacket and tartan waistcoat sitting at a table browsing through a pile of books. Susie moved towards the shelf to get a better look. The books were mainly charted arrivals, departures and casualties covering exotic places; Sydney, Adelaide, Hong Kong, Bombay. They spent half an hour just looking through, trying to get a picture of the expanse of the trade routes.

Finally Susie suggested coffee which automatically came

with pastries this time and picked up a couple of newspapers on her way to their seats. A couple of men near the door glanced up at her. She looked slightly different from the local women, despite feeling like a wreck inside, but it wasn't that. It occurred to her that most probably women weren't allowed to be in these types of places, these rooms were solely occupied by men, but nobody seemed to object, and no one had tried to throw her out exactly. She passed a paper with plain text to Jude, keeping the illustrated copy for herself. The stories weren't dissimilar to the papers they were used to, there were still attention grabbing headlines all over the front cover, but not excessively alluring. 'Well, we're up to date with the news and the coffee tasted better,' said Susie. 'Yeah, are you ready to go?' asked Jude. Susie nodded and they made their way outside.

Assuming they would get a better price for the charms in the west of London, they began walking in that general direction. As they approached the end of a passage on a wider road they could see a few omnibuses each being drawn by two horses. It looked like most of the passengers sat at the top whilst the two drivers sat at the lower level and a few others sat behind them. The bus contained mostly office clerks and other workers wearing stove-pipe hats, but no labourers. 'Come on, let's catch a bus,' suggested Jude. They thought it was quite expensive, but it would give them a different perspective, so they got on board by starting to climb the exterior ladder hoping to sit sideways like everybody else. However they quickly noticed that there were no women up there, so they retreated and went and sat inside below. There was no getting away from the smells here either, thought Susie and partially covered her nose.

In small writing at the front of the bus read '*The French General Omnibus Company*', and the green sign dangling from the side of the bus said '*drives between Euston and Chelsea, sixpence to a shilling*'. They knew that a shilling could feed a family for a week, so the difference between the poor and the wealthier was already becoming glaringly obvious. The conductor banged on the roof, making Jude jump, and the omnibus moved on. It shuffled slowly amongst the hordes of other types of vehicles and the walkers, all mingling together.

The slow, jerky ride soon sent Susie into a trance and she thought about how the whole of London was beginning to smell like the stables and how she couldn't get the smell out of her nostrils; although amazingly she was slowly adjusting to it. She thought about all the public waste going directly into the Thames and the water supply that was coming directly from it, hence the disgusting brownish colour. She gulped and reminded herself not to drink it. She pondered about the Great Stink. She knew from her history lessons that it would occur in only a few years' time, when the suffocating smell of excrement in the Thames nearly chokes the people in the Houses of Parliament. The situation becomes so bad that the politicians have to hang strips of cloth the size of sheets covered in chloride of lime to absorb it. It was strange; even though the crux of the problem is brought right to their door and they can't possibly ignore it any longer, the situation only begins to improve when the impressive sewerage is eventually built. She looked at the other passengers and wondered how they could put up with the awful state of affairs; they were living in one of the most advanced countries in the world, yet it was also one of the most backward; she was sure that in other parts of the world they had mastered the art of purifying water years ago. Yes, they must drink something else; she would have to try gin and ale, which appeared to be what most people were drinking anyway.

There were about three lanes thick with traffic keeping to the left and the same amount coming in the other direction. Jude noticed how the buildings looked a brown or olive green colour, almost like the charred effect on a barbecue. Many buildings were blazoned with advertisements for shows, attractions and refreshments, a bit like a latter day *Time Out* for London. People were leaning out of windows and others were crowded on to small balconies, some hanging precariously over the edge. The conductor was yelling most of the time, and continually yelled 'Ba.aa.nk' as the bus edged towards the river and slowed to a halt. It was here that they decided to get off and join the thronging crowds of people and animals. Many of them were standing or heading towards one of the piers where beyond, in the centre of the Thames, could be seen hundreds of steamboats, some of which were docking and depositing a continual flow of people, among them clerks and dock-porters. Jude and Susie stood mesmerised, watching the masses all moving around and wondering where they were all going.

'I don't know about you, but should we just follow the mainstream of people?' asked Susie. 'Yeah, and stay close,' replied Jude. Susie was hovering next to his heels for most of the way until Jude saw a large pawnbroker and they took the opportunity to change a charm. They decided on the little boot, but it was one of Susie's favourites, she had saved up for this one herself and she tried to quell feelings of regret at having to part with her charms at all. When they came out she was soon distracted as they passed by tiny, intricate shops and then more substantial retailers began to appear.

'Let's look in here,' Susie suggested. It appeared to be a small department store. The ladies' section was on the first floor, the men's on the ground, but Jude decided to follow Susie surreptitiously, almost hiding behind her.

'Look at these,' he said pointing to two signs amongst the goods, one saying '*smuggled*' and the other saying '*stolen*'. 'It seems to be written in a rather gratified way, how times have changed.'

Susie acknowledged but was clearly in full shopping swing and was skirting round the store like a professional. 'I need to get some more petticoats to fill out my dress and maybe some bloomers, just something to show I blend in better with the public.'

'Okay – why don't you get one of these as well?' he said, pointing to a triangular looking shawl. 'A lot of the women are wearing these.'

'I suppose,' said Susie, almost frowning at the old-fashioned look she was trying to achieve but really wanted to avoid. She selected the items, took them over to the counter and handed over a sovereign. For some reason the shopkeeper took it and bounced it on the glass, placing his ear close to it as if he was listening for a special sound. Seemingly satisfied he then held it in his palm and tossed it lightly into the air, caught it and then passed it on to a younger man, with a distinct family resemblance, who disappeared round the back fleetingly and returned with the change.

'They probably don't trust anyone,' said Jude, looking round as though all those in the shop were villains. Once outside Susie pulled Jude into a side street and asked him to keep watch while she put the layers on straight away. It instantly lifted the dress into a fitting style more suitable for that year than the straight drop it had had before.

'Right, what's next – shall we try and walk towards the Strand?' suggested Jude. He was as keen and excited as Susie. Everything was such a novelty; he couldn't take it all in. He felt that he should be constantly worried about getting back, but somehow he felt entranced by the sheer liveliness of it all. Although the place was heaving with activity, there were more open spaces here than in the London he had grown up with. Many of the buildings so familiar to him hadn't even been built yet. This was probably why St. Paul's and Westminster Palace stood out so much. He found it interesting that all classes of people were mingled together, side by side, although he had read that those with money preferred to live on the outskirts of the city, so that they could remove themselves from the obvious plight of the poor. He stared at the crowds and in particular at those more stylishly dressed. These were financially fickle times, though – who knew how long a person's wealth would last.

Susie tugged at his arm, breaking his stream of thought. She guided him off the wide thoroughfare of the Strand through an arcade that was built in a Grecian style. Here there were more children walking with their guardians or parents. There were shops that sold toys, and many were international shops; French, German and Swiss. They all sold interesting trinkets and just a general hodgepodge of curious items that are not necessarily needed. They wandered idly through it and out on to the street again. Straight ahead was a large bazaar and they automatically went inside.

'Careful,' said Jude, pulling Susie out of a man's way. He could already see some unsavoury characters wandering around and assumed they were opportunist pickpockets. Susie wasn't even looking ahead, just upwards. Everything was a wonder around here. There was such a mix of people; this was people watching at its best, but you had to be on your guard. The bazaar had three lanes enclosed by a high glass ceiling. They walked up and down, glancing at all the fancy goods, much of which appeared to be made of leather. Jude noticed a man slide a silver ornament off the edge of a stall and into his inside coat pocket, and then wave a knife at the stallholder when he was about to shout out. He said nothing to Susie; it would only make her panic. But it did remind him of how naive they were so he suggested they split the coins equally between them, in case some got lost or stolen. Susie was less concerned about the money, although she did feel better for having more on her; she was still worried about looking like an outsider. Jude could see she felt uncomfortable, making quick glances over her shoulder and tried to console her.

'Don't forget that half the population of the country are living here in London at the moment, people come and go, they are like ships in the night – two people like us will go unnoticed.' He had a knack of reading her thoughts just by her facial expressions, and she was grateful that she wasn't in this predicament alone.

There was a late afternoon glow as the sun started to set.

'Let's get something to eat shall we?' Susie said, once again overcome by hunger.

'Well there seems to be more choice in this area, so let's try a dining house,' Jude replied. They didn't waste much time. They became absorbed in the energetic atmosphere and there were many places to eat, all offering different prices in varied styles of rooms. They decided on one, went in and sat down. They sat side by side on a high backed bench. Susie noticed the tablecloth was stained, but at least the table was covered. Looking around there were a few posters on the walls and a gas lamp in the small window to the side gave off a warm glow. A waiter came over with a cloth hung over his right arm.

'What will you be wanting,' he said, 'we have roast beef, boiled beef, pork, veal, ham, salmon and shrimp sauce, pigeon pie–' He was droning on in a monotonous tone and by the time he had finished they couldn't remember it all. During his transmission Susie's mind had drifted to a comedy sketch where the waiter recites the list of dishes available in a completely uninterested manner, hinting that the place wasn't worth visiting at all. She pictured her family all sitting together laughing and she giggled to herself and then went serious, obviously deep in thought. She looked up to see Jude and the waiter staring at her dubiously. She had been staring into space and hadn't even noticed the waiter had stopped talking. How long had she been like that? She wanted to laugh out loud, but instead collected her thoughts, 'I'll have roast beef,' she said, 'make that two, and a jug of ale please,' added Jude. The waiter nodded and left.

'Where on earth were you a moment ago?' asked Jude. Susie had been thinking about home and had then reflected on the first time she had become acquainted with Jude. He had always been thoughtful. They had met whilst chatting outside the cinema in small groups and he had offered to walk her and her friend home after they had missed their bus. He spent most of the time with his head tilted upwards, giving them a passionate commentary on the star appellations in the night sky and she couldn't help but notice how different he was.

'Oh, I was just daydreaming,' she replied.

'Starting to feel homesick?' he asked.

'Of course, I love it at home, but I do feel really comfortable here. I can't pinpoint it. It doesn't make any sense.' Jude was worried; a thought occurred to him that she might not want to return with him when the time came. He sensed there was more, and he stared at the floor and waited.

'Imagine staying here – think what an advantage we'd have, knowing all that we know, and look how sociable everyone is. At home if you go out and have a good time you've got to try your best not to get mugged on the way home. Where's the fun in that?'

Jude interrupted, 'Now you're being simplistic. You wouldn't stand a chance here. You would be frowned upon if you took up further study and nothing you own would ever belong to you.' Susie capitulated.

'I know, I was only speculating,' she said, realising how ridiculous she had sounded. Jude smiled and changed the subject.

'We may as well have ale, not sure what else we're supposed to drink.'

'That's fine, I like ale anyway,' said Susie excited and

apprehensive at the same time. 'But I wonder—' she paused as a waiter walked past, 'whether my stomach will cope with all this change in diet.'

The thought hadn't occurred to Jude, he felt that he could eat most things without any bother, 'You'll get used to it, we've got to eat, so as long as we can afford it let's stay around here in the centre where things seem to at least resemble food and drink,' he replied. Just then the beer arrived. They both stared at the grimy glasses and then drank quickly at first, as if to get it over with, but steadied their pace as they began to relax a little and contemplate their strange situation.

CHAPTER FOUR

The day was fading and the pink hue of the sky was slowly sliding into an early evening light. Jude and Susie had had plenty to eat and decided that tomorrow they would try and find other places frequented by the wealthier types. Meanwhile Jude had previously noticed a small exhibition of cosmoramic pictures, called the 'Magic Cave' in the Strand. He was curious to know whether there were any images of the universe or if they were merely scenic pictures of exotic locations. He persuaded Susie to go back there and make this their next stop. As they got nearer they could see the price advertised as one shilling each to enter. They paid up and once inside Jude suggested that they sit and try to work out the currency. There were so many coins, too. They had heard of pounds, shillings and pence but some of them had two names, and then there were crowns, florins, groats, and so it went on. They had sat and figured out that £1 equalled 240 pence here, which made it even harder to work the sums out. But they knew that the crown and half-crown were both silver and that the sovereign and the half were gold. Susie was starting to despair but Jude was becoming good at placating them both, partly because he could see how easily they could spiral into unnecessary worry about almost everything. He told her to compare themselves to the many foreigners he had seen passing through London, assuring her that they were exactly the same when deliberating over which coins to use. Susie was listening but was keen to move on, excitedly inspecting their surroundings.

'Wow, look in here,' she exclaimed. Jude wished she would

just slow down but went over to join her. She was looking at the colourful pictures displayed all around the sides of the cave. They appeared to be mainly oil paintings placed behind a lookalike window, but the panes were convex lenses which altered the appearance and perspective. The pictures had black frames around them and were illuminated by lamps above. There were mainly images of landmarks of other countries and various objects of cosmic interest. Another older looking display was named a Showbox, which was similar but the views were of British landscapes in oil on glass. The panes were movable and lit by candles at the back. Susie looked through the magnifying lens to view the captivating moonlit scenes. The displays were all open for people to look at and touch and there were benches dotted around for visitors to sit and take in the views. They both sat.

'Hey look, that must be Venice, it looks as beautiful as ever,' Susie said.

'Oh yeah, and where's that?' replied Jude. It was a picture of Paris minus the Eiffel Tower, so it took them a while to work it out. Then without warning Jude began to feel slightly claustrophobic; he started to question the reality of their situation and felt an urgent need to get out into the open air. He forgot about Susie and ran to the exit. He closed his eyes, took a deep breath and counted to five as he exhaled. Susie caught up with him. She had known him for two years now, since they began the history course, but she had never seen him like this. Sensing his anxiety she tried to think of a way to distract him.

'I know it's smoky out here, but maybe we can sit a moment and look up at the stars. Can you imagine it, without any electricity to blind our views?' she said.

Jude smiled. 'Yeah, let's do that now.' They stepped across the street again and he cradled her hand with his; he had hated that feeling in the cave and was grateful that she was sympathetic. He pulled her sideways towards a couple of wooden sleepers and they sat down and stared up. He took another deep breath and felt a lot better. Then they both tilted their heads upwards; it was difficult to see anything at first, the smog was patchy and they needed to try to look beyond it. They patiently watched clouds swirling past and in between were patches of clear sky.

'Wow,' he said. 'Look at that.' The sky was momentarily crammed with bright, twinkling stars.

'Unbelievable,' agreed Susie.

'Even better,' said Jude as he got up and starting marching towards something he had seen in the distance. In his excitement he left Susie behind, but she scrambled up and charged after him. Across the street a man was standing beside a very large telescope. He was charging a penny to look through and a sign was hung nearby saying '*view of moon*'. Jude wandered up to him, paid him and tried to look through.

'No, no you need to stand on this stool,' said the man pushing it towards him. Jude stepped up and got a proper view.

'Wow, look at this!' he shouted over to Susie. 'It's incredible, such a clear view. There's millions and millions of stars, look at the constellations. I wish I had my camera to take a photograph and capture it.'

Susie ran over, 'Shh–' she found herself saying again, 'stop shouting things out that other people might not understand.'

'Sorry,' said Jude more quietly, 'but come and have a look.'

'Oi, that'll be another penny, pal,' said the man.

'Yes, of course,' said Jude and paid up. Then Susie stepped up to have a look. It was amazing and she understood why he was so excited and as they walked off they became wrapped up in a discussion about the positioning of the stars.

'Shall we walk towards our lodgings and then just go to a pub?' Jude asked.

'I suppose – but have you noticed that the people spilling

out of them seem a bit tipsy?'

'Don't worry; we'll sit near the entrance ready for a quick exit.' With that they decided to go into the friendliest looking pub they could find. Inside there were all types of characters. Women were openly welcomed here, although looking around Susie could definitely see more men. The bar looked very similar to those in their own time and actually they were used to being surrounded by drunken people, at least at weekends.

'What'll it be?' asked the bartender.

'A tall glass of ale,' replied Jude. 'And I'll have gin, please,' Susie added.

The bartender sighed.

'Will that be a quart, half or pint of gin?'

'What? Oh, no I can't drink that much,' replied Susie raising her eyebrows as she looked at Jude. The bartender stared at her and there was an awkward silence until he spoke again,

'Look, I'll give ya a pennyworth,' he said and then added, 'do you want peppermint with it?' Susie thought this sounded revolting, but nodded.

'Yes please.' She wasn't sure what she wanted but knew it wasn't this; however she was determined not to cause a fuss. Slightly perplexed, they sat down.

'I don't understand, why the big measures?' asked Susie.

'I don't know – they seem to be pouring gin from big jugs as though it was ale. I guess it keeps everyone going, but I can't imagine not being able to drink water. Anyway, if you think about it they are the same measures that they give in European holiday resorts,' he said smiling and trying to make light of it. Although looking at Susie's gin, he was shocked at how generous a measure it was. 'Just go easy,' he cautioned.

They took small sips and looked around. Jude couldn't believe how tired he was. It made him realise how little exercise he got at home. He was a keen footballer and played for a local team, but walking for what seemed like miles each day was something else. Towards the corner of the bar a few people seemed to be gently swaying and one man was actually perched on the bar. Drinks were being spilled everywhere as people moved around the floor with their overflowing tankards. He noticed a young girl walk in, no smiles, looking straight ahead and carrying a large jug. The bartender filled it up and she hurriedly took it straight out again, presumably to her parents, he thought. Over to the left of them a group of people were talking and staggering and they cringed when they saw one man actually lying down on the floor, cursing at no one in particular.

Trying to ignore him, Susie and Jude started up a stilted conversation. Susie explained that she was particularly interested in the lives of all the French chefs who had come to London. She wanted to see if she could sneak into one of the kitchens somehow and find out how things were done. This was one of her favourite pastimes. She lived with her parents and younger sister and was always cooking in her spare time.

She turned to Jude hesitantly, not sure how he would respond.

'Did you know I own a few Victorian cookbooks?' His mouth started to curl into a smile, 'Really?' he replied.

'Yes, I've got one by Eliza Acton, and one by Alexis Soyer, the French chef.'

'Who?' asked Jude, having never heard of this obscure character.

'He was a French chef, way ahead of his time, I think. Apart from the chefs, not many people in this time period seemed to know how to cook – he even went into people's homes and watched them cook so that he could help them do it better or more economically.' She began pointing, ' you can see just from looking around – nobody is cooking, they're either eating on the street or taking their meat to communal ovens in chop houses like that one over there and having it cooked for them. I bet they sometimes even come out with someone else's dinner.'

'Well, you do surprise me, what about Mrs. Beeton then?'

'Her cookbook came out a bit later I think. Anyway they were mostly recipes that everyone else had sent in, plus recipes from other chefs, including Alexis Soyer. But what really went down well was all Mrs. Beeton's advice about running a home, because not many people could.'

'Scintillating stuff,' he said teasingly and she jokingly shoved him away from her. Just then a man stumbled towards the bar, ordered a drink and turned to stare at them. He was quite tall compared to others and had dark hair and brown eyes, and was wearing an old long coat. He looked a bit dishevelled and was quite moody looking. Jude felt immediately uncomfortable, like he'd been caught red handed, but then realised the man was actually staring at Susie in a lustful way. He was staring at her boots and then at the hem of her dress, his eyes seemed to be moving slowly upwards. Susie had noticed, but looked down, staring at her hands awkwardly. He just wouldn't look away, making her feel strangely violated. Without warning Jude suddenly jumped up and walked over to him. Susie noticed he wasn't exactly walking in a straight line, they had both had quite a lot to drink, but before she knew it Jude had pushed the man in the chest shouting 'don't you know it's rude to stare?' She panicked and started to get up, feeling a little unsteady herself, but before she could do anything Jude was flying backwards past her and landed in a heap amongst some stools. She ran over to him.

'Jude, are you alright, whatever were you doing?'

He winced and rubbed the back of his head.

'I don't know, everyone in here just seems so uncouth and unkempt, the creep just got to me,' he said.

'Never mind, let's just get up slowly and get out of here.'

She helped him up and they crept out with their heads down, hoping nobody else would pick on them. She heard the man mutter 'stupid swell,' but purposefully ignored him and guided Jude out.

It was almost pitch black outside now. A few gas lamps in windows lit the way, but if they ventured further out it would be hopeless. Susie was tripping and stumbling on the cobblestones, it was infuriating trying to walk on uneven pavement, especially at night. As if the stones weren't bad enough she was also slipping on mud, or excrement by the smell of it, made worse by the amount of people shuffling past, spilling drinks and turning the area into a quagmire. She felt really fed up but was determined not to be defeated by it and had to try and stay cheerful after what had happened. She turned to Jude.

'Thanks for looking out for me, but you've got to be careful. Are you okay now?' Jude was still rubbing his head but said he was fine and they kept going, each alone with their thoughts. There was a lengthy silence.

'What's up?' asked Jude.

'Oh, nothing,' she smiled bravely, 'just thinking about the eating places I'd like to visit in town and how I would love to have a peek into their kitchens,' she replied, trying to make conversation and appear lighter hearted than she actually felt.

'That's feasible; I could pretend to be a lurker and write a note saying you need a job: "My Dearest Patisserie King, I suggest you help this young lady as she is out of money and needs to practise her skills in mille-feuille—" '

'Very funny, but that's not a bad idea,' she laughed. 'What about you, what are you interested in while you're here?'

'I wouldn't mind trying to find a football match and seeing what they're like. I think the rules will be different, but I bet they're passionate about it,' replied Jude.

'Well one thing I don't want to see is a public execution,

even though it's supposed to be a family event, picnic included.'

'I don't think they do that anymore, that was eighteenth century, surely, but I think they were held on Mondays; no idea if it's the same now, but keep a look out just in case,' he teased.

Susie wasn't sure how serious he was being so she changed the subject to entertainment and they both agreed they also wanted to sample the night life, from a safe distance if possible after tonight, and thought that the Haymarket would be a cool place to hang out judging by Davy's commentary on how vibrant the night life was. First thing tomorrow, though, they needed more money. Feeling weary, the conversation lessened and they both concentrated on retracing their steps back to their room in Holborn.

CHAPTER FIVE

The next morning they arose to the same sights and sounds. By all accounts this must be Tuesday, thought Jude. He looked at his watch which was still working, amazingly, and tucked it back into a deep pocket. Eight-thirty; it could be one of those trips where you get up later and later each day; then he laughed at the idea that he considered this a trip rather than an ordeal. They got themselves together; making sure they never left anything behind.

'Are you hungry?' he asked Susie.

'Ravenous.'

'Okay, how about going to a breakfast house this morning?'

'Good idea', she replied. They started walking amongst the crowds but went in a different direction to yesterday, keeping away from the general traffic. Their money was low, so they thought they would find an Irish Ordinary. They had already seen quite a few and noticed that the prices were set so it was a good way to keep track of their spending. There was nowhere to sit inside so they did what they observed others doing and ordered the set breakfast of bacon, bread and coffee at 1½d, waited for it to arrive, then took it outside and sat on a step and ate.

'It's funny how many similarities there are to our own time, don't you think?' asked Jude. Susie had finished eating and was leaning on her knees with her coffee cupped in both hands.

'In what way?'

'Just that you can get a quart of beer here for a penny and a cup of coffee for the same price; it's about £3 for a pint of beer and the same for a large cup of frothy coffee at home. The streets are teeming now with walkers and some transport and yet they're really overcrowded with vehicles in our London; look at the congestion charge. And then there's the sooty, choky atmosphere here and the London smog from car fumes. What's the difference?'

'You're getting philosophical all of a sudden,' said Susie, 'but you've got a point. At least it's quieter in our future, though, I think the streets are much noisier here – I can't hear myself think.' She had a sudden longing for winter at home and the profound silence that snow brings.

'True, true,' agreed Jude, who was again thinking about life back at home. He had passed his driving test at eighteen, so in a way he wasn't helping the environment either, although he didn't own a car.

'Anyway,' Susie got up, 'let's find a place to change one of my charms.'

They walked for an hour or so and eventually came to a large pawnbroker shop. They went inside and joined a few other people who were queuing. Some women wore scarves around their head and the usual shawl draped around their shoulders. Men were handing over various things, often made of lead and cast iron. Jude noticed the man behind the counter was surrounded by pots and kettles, spoons and forks and piles of cloth. It looked more like an auction room than a silversmith, but he didn't really care at this point. He saw a sign above a pile of hankies and noticed it said cotton, 6d and silk 6 shillings. Feeling the material around his neck he reassured himself he could fall back on this if he was desperate for cash. Susie gave him one of her charms in the shape of a padlock and when his turn came he handed it to the pawnbroker.

'I've never seen anything like this before,' he exclaimed, moving it between his fingers and holding it away from him as though he was about to begin sketching it. He took another long look at Jude and Susanna which made other people in the crowd turn to stare at them too. They shuffled awkwardly for a moment and then Jude said 'they're more common where we're from, you know, we use them in the country, it's a new kind of lock for those hefty barn doors.' This appeared to be a satisfactory explanation as they were handed a few shillings in return and abruptly left.

'Shall we go to Vauxhall Gardens? They're supposed to be similar to the Tivoli Gardens in Copenhagen,' Susie asked.

'I've never heard of either of them, but I don't see why not.'

'It's only seasonal I think but I'm sure it's on until the end of September.'

'Do you read up on this stuff in your spare time or something?' said Jude who was beginning to wonder what Susie did for fun at home. He never saw her out at clubs in the evening. Perhaps she was born in the wrong era he thought, bemused at the irony of this. As if reading his thoughts Susie added, 'it's just that there's so much going on here. People are making their own entertainment day and night and it's just–'

'Don't feel you have to explain, I'm interested too,' he replied, which was half true.

They realised the best way to get there was by boat from London Bridge. Susie began leading the way, but Jude quickly pulled her back.

'Don't go that way; it's too near Newgate prison. Let's go towards Fleet Street and towards the old city from there.' They weren't in any rush but soon got tired of walking. It seemed like their legs just ached more every day instead of becoming accustomed to it. They carried on, but began to wilt at the sheer mileage they had been clocking up. They went towards the Temple Bar archway.

'Wow,' said Jude, 'Look at this.' He stared at the decorated sides of the arch itself and the large window right in the centre.

It looked like an actual room that was being used. They both craned their necks as they went under it to get a good look but were almost crushed with the volume of people and carts trying to squeeze through at the same time.

'It was considered a bottleneck for the traffic and was taken down in pieces and removed. Then it went to a private manor somewhere outside London, but was recently brought back. I think it's in Paternoster Square now, opposite St. Paul's,' said Susie. They were glad to get out from under the arch.

'Is it? – I can't wait to take a look when we go to London next,' he said and they both had a fit of laughing at how ridiculous this sounded.

'Seriously, though, I am really worn out,' said Jude. But Susie was quick to buck him up, reminding him that Dickens had walked twenty-thirty miles daily, and that unless you were wealthy, most people here walked everywhere. They carried on until they came towards a hospital. They slowed down to see what the people outside were doing. There were three people in a row wearing advertising boards. One was a chiropodist, another appeared to be a self-made pharmacist selling cough drops and the third wore a sign that simply said '*don't go in there*'.

'Charming,' said Jude, 'well hopefully we won't have to.' They both moved swiftly on. Eventually Jude gave in. 'Oh blow this, let's try and call one of those hansom cabs.' There were plenty around. They all had four wheels and were pulled by two horses that generally looked very tired. He hollered for one. The driver looked over in a sneering sort of way. He was stooped over the reins.

'What d'ya want?' he said.

'A ride to London Bridge if you don't mind,' shouted Jude. The noise level was beginning to grate on him. Susie had gone quiet; the men around here were starting to give her the creeps.

'What will you give?' bellowed the driver. He was

aggressive and drunk. Jude handed over a shilling, not having a clue what to give; it was probably too much he thought. The driver told them to get aboard. They both squeezed into the tiny carriage area, it was really claustrophobic, there was barely enough room for two people, but they sat very still and watched the driver's reins dangle right over their heads. They were still in the Fleet Street area and despite the rough ride they both sat quietly in awe of their surroundings. There were even larger advertisements here for Fleet Street newspapers which covered the sides of buildings from top to bottom. People walked carrying their loads, some above their heads, some just slung over their shoulders, but there were hats on everyone's heads. There were plenty of omnibuses on the roads, but ahead for the first time they could see a steam train going over a bridge.

'Look at that,' said Susie as though she had never seen a train before. The journey was slow and long and even though they were in a cab they cringed at the thought of being trampled or fallen on by the throngs of crowds that were sitting in vehicles higher up than them. The familiar sight of St. Paul's cathedral dome was now in the distance, and their skilful chauffeur, who was good at negotiating the winding roads and gaps, was bringing it ever nearer. Eventually they could see London Bridge and gracefully thanked the driver, for what it was worth.

Jude took one look at the mob of people hanging around the steps of the bridge. He took Susie's hand and guided her round them. They joined a small queue of people waiting for boats.

'I'm glad we're getting a boat next, sometimes this town doesn't seem to have any beginning or end,' said Susie.

'I know, it's permanently like moving slowly with the crowds of people leaving at the end of a festival.'

'What do you think those people are doing?' asked Susie

pointing to groups of families standing at the river's edge, some with toddlers in their arms.

'I think they must be mudlarks,' replied Jude and seeing Susie's confused face explained.

'They wait until the tide goes out and then stand in the thick mud and using their toes start hunting for anything left behind by the ships, you know stuff like coal, wood, iron or copper, in fact most of the things we saw in the pawnbrokers, anything they can sell on.'

'Oh dear, I suppose they could use the driftwood to burn in their fires.'

'Yes… I suppose.'

Jude looked at the Thames and wondered what else was lurking in there. He knew that people set out in rowing boats specifically to retrieve whole bodies or body parts to hand over to the police, presumably for money too, but didn't bother mentioning this to Susie in case she changed her mind about getting on the boat.

The river was packed with all kinds of steamboats and barges, all overflowing with people. A small steamboat came to the tiny beach-like area where they were standing in a small queue. Jude and Susie scrambled aboard, and perched on a plank and the boat began gliding slowly across the water. In comparison to the road traffic, the scene was somewhat calmer just from the sound of the flow of the water, although the smell was sickening. Opposite them sat a man and woman sitting amorously together. The woman was perched on the man's knee and her laced chest was nestling in his moustache. They were giggling and tipping a bit, probably drunk thought Susie and she tried not to look. Jude could see a dead cat bobbing up and down in the water which reaffirmed his earlier thoughts and now all he could think of was a brown, dead river full of rotting body parts that must be floating around. He thought that the fish must have given up a long time ago, and reminded himself not to put his hands anywhere near the water.

They passed St. Saviour's Church, only recognising it because of its location, but the surrounding area was totally unbeknown to them. At Waterloo bridge pier Susie could see a toll keeper surrounded by large groups of females hanging around and had a hunch that these were the 'fallen' women so often referred to by politicians and writers of the time. Her understanding of the social history was that despite the unstoppable progress; the scientific discoveries, amazing engineering achievements and creative flair, it was the drunks and the prostitutes that seemed to define the Victorian age and she had begun to notice both more and more. They had been on the river for a couple of hours and Susie felt lulled into a stupor by ripples of water lapping against the boat, despite the hustle and bustle of the Thames. Jude was nudging her.

'Look over there,' he said. On the river's edge was a mass of brickwork, like a fortress. 'I recognise this from old photographs; it's the Millbank Prison, the largest in London.' Susie followed his gaze.

'Gosh it looks like a Tyrolean building, look at those towers with their pointed roofs. You half expect someone like Maid Marion to wave a flag from one of the top windows!' she replied.

'Do you remember who designed it?' asked Jude.

'No, but I've got a feeling you're gonna tell me,' Susie replied.

'Jeremy Bentham,' he said, ignoring her comment. 'Don't you remember Davy talking about Jeremy Bentham's Panopticon?'

'Yes, vaguely.'

'The building is made up of six pentagons around a circular centre which lets the guards see all the prisoners all the time – yet another remarkable invention.'

'You mean just like our modern day CCTV cameras.'

'Exactly,' said Jude. 'By the way the prisoners in there have all been sentenced and are waiting for transportation to Australia.'

'Call that punishment! – Oh, I've just realised where we are,' said Susie, 'this is where the Tate Britain stands, I've been on the Tate to Tate boat tour with my family. We came here for the day – this is so weird.'

'I wish he was here now to share all this,' said Jude.

'Who?'

'Davy,' he said, 'he always encouraged us to try and imagine being in the historical place at the time, you know by trying to imagine all the smells and sounds.' They both went quiet and momentarily missed home and college for that matter.

Before long they were approaching Vauxhall Bridge. When they got off the boat they went straight to Vauxhall Gardens, which wasn't far as they could already see posters dotted around leading to the entrance. The posters read '*World's Fair – not open weekends – season closes 23rd September*'; some of them were in English and some in French. The entrance fee was a shilling but if you were going in on a balloon ascent night it would have been 1s 6d. In smaller print Jude noticed that although the Gardens were open to the public the main attractions were in the evening. They had been on the move for hours but thought it would be better to come back later, and retraced their steps until they found the hot potato stand they had passed and joined the queue. When it was their turn they were each handed one with butter and they found a quieter area to sit and waited for them to cool down. They could see the action on the river but were far enough away from the stench. Jude bit into his potato with his teeth and surveyed the scene.

'There are so many boats; I reckon you could use them as

stepping stones to get to the other side.' Susie laughed, 'Yeah, if you were a giant, maybe.' They finished their food and leaned back, listening to the sounds of creaking sails and masts and of wooden crates being bandied about. The afternoon was warm and when the sun finally shone through they dozed lightly for a few hours, opening their eyes every so often to check that they were safe.

Susie sat up first and then leaned on her elbow. She realised it was calmer in general around here; they were still in the town but it felt much more suburban. It was spacious and slightly greener and she thought it must be why people were coming here in their droves. She looked down at Jude and thought he actually looked quite peaceful, she leant a little closer to him and noticed how beautiful his long eyelashes were. She nudged him gently to wake him, as there were more and more people walking past, all dressed in their finery and all heading in the direction of Vauxhall Gardens. He sat up instantly as if he had heard a gun being fired. Susie felt sorry for him; it just showed how on edge they both were all the time, always having to watch their back, almost waiting to be accosted. He was blinking repeatedly, trying to adjust his eyes to the daylight.

'Is it time to go? Are they open?' he asked.

'Yes, I think so; I've seen hundreds of people walk past.'

'Okay, let's go.' Jude got up. He was keen to get moving again and they joined the growing crowds. Susie had a better look around this time. The wharfs around the river had a nautical feel, boats, warehouses and jetties were all scattered on the quaysides. Adjacent were the backs of tall, terraced houses with balcony areas. She realised that this was the time of evening she liked most, just like an evening stroll whilst on holiday as the sun was setting. She looked to her left and could see open fields in the distance and sheep grazing. No wooden scaffolding in sight. 'Look at that,' she pointed, showing Jude, 'it's so nice to finally see the edges of this massive city, or should I say construction site as usually all you can hear are sounds of demolition!'

Again they approached the gates of Vauxhall Gardens and entered along with other families. As they walked in they could see row upon row of tree-lined avenues and boxes, like modern day booths, all curving round in a horseshoe, each one having a table inside where people were stopping for food and drink. All around were small stalls set out in no particular order, which made it more enticing, and as it was noticeable how much was being done for charity, it was also like being at a fete. They purposely went to the stalls that had signs that read '*in aid of*' and '*for the relief of*' and then Jude had a go in the Shooting Gallery. After that they walked towards an American Bowling Saloon, decorated on the outside with a panorama of the USA. 'Let's go in there and get a drink,' he said. They decided to try the Mint Juleps. They watched as the barman mixed ice with sugar and then added brandy, rum and lemon rind. He shook it, poured the mixture into two dainty glasses and finished by adding a sprig of mint. He passed them a stick of macaroni each.

'What are we supposed to do with these?' asked Susie, puzzled.

'I think they are meant to be straws. Just drink through them,' replied Jude. The drinks were delicious compared with some they had previously tried and without hesitation they asked for two more. The place certainly had an international feel about it and they sat for a while enjoying it enormously. Leaving the Saloon they saw that nearby was a huge panoramic Swiss landscape with a Tyrolean vocalist standing underneath dressed in full native costume, yodelling.

'He should be standing outside Millbank prison,' joked Susie. Just then somebody barged into her ripping part of her lace sleeve off.

'What on earth was that?' she said shakily. Jude grabbed her wrist, 'I think she must have been trying to grab your bracelet.' He pulled her towards the grass verge where they took off the bracelet and she quickly buried it in her top jacket pocket. 'We'll have to be more careful,' said Jude, 'keep your wits about you.'

They tried not to let it spoil the atmosphere, but decided to walk more quickly; even though now they had nothing on show worth stealing. They passed all kinds of plants, labelled rare and exotic, which were mostly situated on raised flower beds and running down slopes. After a while they stopped and stood behind a crowd, wondering what all the squeals of delight were, Jude wandered over first.

'Look at this,' he said. He was pointing to an exhibit which was showcasing some kind of engineering. He read aloud '*Hydraulic Engineer to the ex-court of Versailles – fire and water sports*'. They sat down and watched a display which they thought would have been interesting even in their time. When the demonstration was over they could hear people discussing food and where to buy tickets. They eavesdropped and followed a few others to a stand that was selling tickets for supper. They bought two tickets and were told they would have to find a seat straight away as the food would be brought out soon. Hundreds of people were sitting down at once and they found a space and squeezed in. The buffet wasn't cheap but everyone was given a bottle of claret with their meal, which consisted of cold chicken and salad and a selection of side dishes as well as bread and cheese. The weather wasn't particularly cold and there were singers dotted around which made it feel like an open air picnic concert.

They sat and watched the other groups of people clearly enjoying themselves. Jude noticed again how the delights of dining al fresco were apparent and turned to Susie.

'Do you know what I like most about this?' Susie glanced

sideways at him and shrugged, she was helping herself to some kind of salad.

'It's a cross between a festival and a fair. You never know what you're going to walk past next.' Susie picked up her wine, 'well, yes, but it seems to be like that in most of the main streets.'

'That's only because we're not used to it; this must be like a mini-holiday to these people; they can get away from the crowds and the relentless spiral of death and disease, even if for a few short hours.'

Susie thought he was being a little melancholic, but she knew what he meant.

'I felt the same when my parents used to take us for days out, you know the kind of thing; playing ball games, hiring rowing boats, picnics, everyone just enjoying the moment and being outdoors.'

Jude was nodding in agreement. 'Yeah, time doesn't matter – until you have to pack your stuff up and head back to reality.'

Susie noticed that this was the second time he had put a downer on their life back home; it sounded like he was getting a bit mixed up. She hoped that he wasn't becoming overly sentimental, talking like they belonged here.

'Try not to get too wrapped up with these people, there's no point, it's not as if we're never going home.'

Jude almost appeared dismayed at this and she realised her apprehension was justified, so she tried to snap him out of it by appealing to his creative side. She became animated.

'Just think of the memoirs we could write when we get home – maybe we could set up a Tour Operation, '*Time for a Change*' we could call it.'

Jude thought about her relentless commentary when they passed something interesting and smiled at the thought of her being a Tour Guide. He reverted back to his normal upbeat self. He chinked his glass against hers, 'well, we're here now so who better to check it all out and report back than us?'

The dishes were cleared and two types of desserts followed which were mainly fruit tarts and various cheesecakes. The atmosphere was lively, it was just like a banquet and they stayed as long as everyone else.

When they moved back into the main grassed aisle lamps were being lit simultaneously around the park, which instantly gave out a party feel. They were drawn to a structure similar to that of a helter-skelter. It was bright and cheery with the shape of a crown at the top. An orchestra was placed on the second level and it sounded as though they had started playing. Beneath at the front was a large area, partially fenced off where a few children were charging about trying out the dance floor but as couples drifted on to it and started dancing they gracefully glided to the sides and stood and watched. Jude and Susie did the same and Jude was relieved she didn't ask him to dance – he wasn't sorry that he was going to miss a chance to make a fool of himself on the dance floor.

Before leaving the park they saw signs for '*The Avenue of all Nations*' and decided to venture down it. Looking around Susie thought that most people here seemed fashionable and well dressed, a different crowd to those they had mostly seen since arriving, but vagrants could still be seen skulking around amongst the strollers. They continued through and then stopped near a man who was introducing some electric lighting. All the while he was watching, Jude was trying to stop himself from interrupting but then he just couldn't resist it. 'Keep going, keep going – you never know what you'll discover next – wait for the light bulb.' Susie dragged him away. 'Shh, don't be so stupid, you'll draw attention to us.' People standing around had begun staring at them instead of the demonstrator and Susie became agitated and suggested that they leave; she was worried that his emotional swings were brought on by the wine.

They went towards the direction of Lambeth and could see to their right that the circus was in town. 'Maybe it's permanently in town,' said Jude noticing the external wooden structure with only the roof made from canvas, 'there's certainly no lack of entertainment around here.' He was aware that he had annoyed Susie and thought that she didn't deserve it. He felt like he was on an emotional roller coaster and made a point of trying to remain positive. They crept towards the large structure and peeped inside. The show had already begun. They didn't want to spend any more money so hid in the shadows of the tent and tried to see what was going on. They could see someone dressed as a clown and trumpets had started to play. Then there was the sound of fast hooves and troops of men on horseback patrolled round the circumference of the inner circle before lining up and retrieving a mock sword from the ringleader. Some of the horses had bright coloured robes over their backs. It was beginning to look like a battle. Sure enough they split into opposite ends and began synchronised charging. Some men fell off their horses, slowly for effect, to the 'oohs and aahs' of the audience. The atmosphere was highly charged and they stayed until the end of the battle which to them was awesome, and then decided to go back towards London Bridge. There didn't appear to be any other way; all moving traffic south of the river seemed to go over it.

In the near distance to the left Jude noticed a suspension bridge leading towards the Hungerford market. The centre of the bridge appeared quite high above the water and the chains were doubled where the suspension rods were attached. He pointed it out to Susie, 'another engineering work of art, look, it's just like the Clifton suspension bridge.' He looked at it again. 'Maybe it was here first and then the chains were moved to Bristol further on in the future.' Susie nodded.

'It's like London Bridge – that was dismantled and re-assembled in Arizona.'

'Yeah, I know – and what about Marble Arch, it was moved from Buckingham Palace wasn't it?'

'I'm not sure,' said Susie shrugging.

'It stands next to where they used to hang people, at Tyburn,' said Jude.

Susie gave him a sideward glance, mumbling 'how come the conversation keeps going back to execution.' She had tried to make light of it, but shivered at the thought, and they both stood still, bewildered by the ever changing past.

CHAPTER SIX

It was late evening and Jude suggested they find a pub. Susie agreed and they began walking towards Kennington. There were still a few costermongers around. Some had small wagons and others donkey and carts, one girl was selling nutmeg graters and a man was selling fresh pineapples close by. It seemed like a lot of goods came easily to London, and there was a distinct international feel; all around she could hear foreign accents and this particular area seemed much more salubrious to them. More street music was playing gently and Jude spotted a nice looking tavern.

Most establishments they had visited in London so far had seemed dark and dank, but this place felt warm and was quite brightly lit, with gas lamps hanging like chandeliers from the ceiling. Behind the bar a man and woman, presumably husband and wife, were serving. There were large signs propped up against the bar showing wine lists and house ales available and there were large barrels behind the bar, right at the back, and old tankards were piled up at the front. They sat down near a window again. Jude decided to ignore the list of alcoholic drinks and instead they both chose to have soft drinks in the hope that they would quench their thirst.

While Jude was at the bar Susie looked around. This definitely felt better. The crowd wasn't so rowdy and there were some people in the corner playing dominoes. They sipped their drinks and watched the usual pantomime of people staggering about, spilling their drinks. Jude noticed a battered old Backgammon set on the other side of the room and went and picked it up. He dusted it off with his sleeve, it looked well used. A large spider appeared on the corner of the box, which made him jump, but he quickly flicked it off and didn't mention it to Susie, knowing how she felt about them. When he brought it back to their table Susie said she didn't know how to play, so Jude explained the rules, taking a break to order more soft drinks, and they played for an hour or so and then decided to move on. It was dark now, so they tried to stay close to the gas lamps which had a fan-shaped flame and weren't particularly bright. The streets were still quite noisy but sounds were more muffled than in the daytime.

Realising they were passing through the Borough district towards Southwick they became vaguely aware of their bearings. Jude noticed it first, The George Inn, the only remaining inn with a gallery dating back to the seventeenth century. Jude, Susie and a group of other college friends had gone on a trip to London organised by Davy who had pointed out the inn to them. It was just before lunchtime then and the inn had looked shut, but they had peered in the small windows and seen that it was like a museum inside. Susie remembered thinking that it looked very dark and spooky. Original clay pots and other ornaments had stood on recessed shelves to the right. The seats and tables were all dated, looking much older than the Victorian era.

'Come on, it's open,' said Jude excitedly. Susie followed behind with slight trepidation. A horse and carriage had pulled up outside and people were cheerily disembarking and entering the inn, relieved at the pause in their journey. At the bar Susie had ordered wine, which tasted of rhubarb and Jude kept to his usual ale. They sat in the centre of the inn as the outer tables were taken up by the travellers. Susie took another gulp of wine and glanced round the room. Her eyes focused on a man sitting opposite her right at the back of the inn. Unbeknown to her he had been watching her since she had entered the room. He looked as though he wasn't with anyone and was dressed unusually; he had a flamboyant white lace collar shirt with lace cuffs underneath a pale grey fitted suit and his hair was tied back with a ribbon. His eyes were green and his hair was fair. Susie was mesmerised by him and his startling good looks and hurriedly guzzled her wine.

She tried to divert her gaze and concentrate on someone else, then turned to Jude and listened to him talking enthusiastically, trying to guess what all the people in the pub did for a living. He was focusing on an elderly gentleman with a newspaper in his hands, scanning it purposefully. He guessed he was some kind of engineer who probably gave talks on machinery in one of the arcades in the West End. Susie glanced back at the man opposite her, but he was gone. Suddenly she felt a hand over her mouth and the weight of someone's body pressing down on her, pushing her backwards into her seat. She tried to scream, but no sound was coming out. She looked over at Jude who seemed oblivious and was staring at his tankard of beer. She furiously flung her arms around trying to push the invisible man off and then suddenly he was gone. In an instant she was free of the weight and had found her voice.

'What on earth was that?' she yelled in shock. Jude was startled and looked at her incredulously.

'Why are you yelling like that?' but Susie had already got up, tilting the table in her hurry to find the exit. She needed fresh air.

'Susie, what's wrong?' asked Jude, running after her.

'I can't describe it, but something or someone, who was invisible to you all by the way, climbed on top of me and wouldn't let go.'

'Okay, calm down, I did sense that you were about to nod off in there. At one point you had your eyes shut and jumped as though you were dreaming. Then I tasted your wine and boy it was so strong it nearly knocked my socks off!'

Susie felt a little calmer after that. It could have been her imagination, she had probably dozed off, but he had seemed so real. She looked at Jude.

'Did you see the gentleman in the grey suit back there? His hair was tied up in a ribbon and he was sitting opposite us, but quite far away?' Jude tried to think but shook his head negatively.

'No, can't say that I did – I think I would have remembered someone of that description; then again there were so many people in there.... why?'

'Oh, I don't know – just remind me not to drink rhubarb wine again, I think it's intoxicating.' She couldn't actually explain what had happened and despite feeling unsettled, she knew she couldn't afford to dwell on it.

They sat on the kerbside in silence until Susie composed herself and then they got up and carried on walking further into Southwark.

There were army barracks nearby and it was noticeable how many groups of women just appeared to be hanging around. Some looked scruffier than others and were very loud and crude, shouting out at gentlemen as they walked by. Susie already felt uneasy and didn't need this so she walked quickly on and without realising was slightly ahead of Jude. When he didn't respond to her question she spun round to see him disappear down an alleyway. She quickly followed, but stood back when she saw that he was surrounded by three women. Two were taunting him whilst the third was desperately rifling through his pockets. She heard one of the women ask him where he lived and would he like to take her home. Jude looked stunned as the first woman was now trying to take his jacket off and the second was trying to kiss him.

'It'll only cost ya a bob,' she said.

'I haven't got any money,' replied Jude, wincing and trying to move his head out of the way.

'Doesn't matter, come here, handsome,' said another, yanking him towards her. Susie's initial shock turned into anger and, horrified, she ran towards them and lunged at them.

'Get off him,' she said taking a swipe at the nearest woman, pulling her hair and knocking her cap off her head.

'Who do you think you are?' cursed the main conspirator and pushed Susie on to the ground. She jumped up straight away and slammed her body into the woman who was mauling Jude. Meanwhile Jude seemed to regain his strength and barged his way out of the group, pulling Susie away with him. They ran as quick as they could until they were sure they had disappeared from view and found themselves in a well-lit side street. Here they slowed down and tried to appear calm as they stepped into the quaint little street with its Tudor houses on both sides. The pace here was considerably slower; there was not much going on apart from the odd stationary horse and cart hanging around quietly beside the houses. Looking above there were attic dwellers with washing hanging out on poles, which made the cobblestones slippery, and some houses had cages with songbirds in hanging outside. Susie stood still for a moment, making Jude pause as well. She was frowning.

'This is a nice reprieve, but what on earth happened there?'

'They came from nowhere; I didn't encourage them at all,' said Jude in his defence. He couldn't look at her as he felt slightly embarrassed, 'that must have been one of the notorious prostitute districts – anyway thank you.' His voice trailed off, he wasn't used to being pounced on like that, the women were surprisingly strong and he was clearly outnumbered. He held Susie's hand, deciding that it would be better to stay close as they journeyed back to their room. They manoeuvred their way over London Bridge, which was a lot easier at this time of night, and walked for what seemed like hours.

It had started to drizzle and Jude took out his watch and

announced that the time was two o'clock in the morning, and suggested that they stop off at a coffee house to get out of it and take a break. Inside it was more like a diner and was dark but cosy and there were a few nomads sitting around also drinking coffee. Perhaps this was the answer to homelessness, thought Jude, a place where one could go at any time of night and get a hot drink for a penny. Susie had taken her cape off and was wrapping her shawl tighter around her shoulders for comfort. He looked at her in a slightly defeated way.

'That was a close call. We're learning the hard way. We've got to be more alert. I'm just not used to be constantly confronted like this – and did you know that the man in the bazaar that I steered you away from had his hand on your waist, aiming for the pocket in your cape?'

'I didn't know that,' said Susie.

'I didn't say anything at the time but we need to treat everyone we encounter as a potential thief I'm afraid.'

'What's new – it's like that at home isn't it? You can't put anything you own down for a minute without it being swiped.'

'Not always,' said Jude who sensed her despondency and wasn't in the mood for an argument. He steered them back to the present.

'It's just that each time it happens, I'm not expecting it, especially the violence – but we should remember that groups of women are either working for men or for themselves and mostly they rob.' Susie sighed and Jude squeezed her hand, they needed to pull together if they were going to get through this.

'Oh come on; let's just forget about it for now,' he said.

They had finished their drinks a while ago so they got up and continued on the last part of their journey back. The rain was coming down harder and Susie pulled her blouse up higher to stop it creeping down the back of her neck.

'I can't wait to lie down, even though it's only on the floor. At least it's dry and private,' she said as they started to jog. Jude shivered, but he knew the way better than Susie, and he stayed close to the buildings until he recognised the small glove shop that was a few doors down from the house where they rented the room. Once inside they laid their outer clothes out flat to dry and collapsed into their own quarters.

CHAPTER SEVEN

They awoke the next day, but this time it was quieter. Jude looked at his watch. 'Blimey, we've been asleep for ages. It's eleven-thirty.' He looked out the window and saw that the street was slightly less busy than usual.

'Okay, another day – let's make the most of it,' he said smiling. 'I think we should try and get to The Great Exhibition – it's the one thing we both really want to see, and then try and find our way home. What do you say?'

'Sounds like a good idea,' replied Susie, 'but I'm sure it's in Hyde Park and that's quite far from here. Can we get an omnibus again; my feet are aching just at the thought of walking.'

'Alright, but I suggest as soon as we get off we change another charm.'

Susie checked her pockets and realised she didn't have much money left at all. She pulled her bracelet from her pocket and showed Jude her last two charms.

'These are all I've got left, the telephone and the silver cat,' she said. He looked at them, 'we're getting through the money quickly aren't we? I just hope it will be enough to get us a ticket into the Exhibition and a ride back to Eva's house. It's not too far to walk from there.'

They made their way outside. It was lunchtime and the streets were becoming busy again. They passed an establishment called The Holborn Restaurant and saw that it was offering turtle soup, and pigeon – both very popular dishes, but they wanted something less grandiose to eat. There were many stalls around. The popular choice appeared to be hot eels, not pickled or jellied, just plain fish with the skin taken off and one man was drinking the cooking liquor to accompany it.

'Seeing him makes me want some fish, but not eels,' said Jude, openly cringing.

'Do you ever feel like we're always at a food court in an enormous shopping centre?' asked Susie. Jude stared at her.

'Obviously not,' she muttered to herself and then added loudly, 'yeah, I'm happy to have fish.'

They stopped at the nearest pub that was offering fish and wandered over to the bar. This time Susie noticed some different soft drinks on offer. Jude was watching her; he thought she looked dishevelled, but lovely.

'Looks like you choose a piece of fish and they fry it for you. Comes with bread and butter.'

'Okay, cool,' she replied and noticed a woman look round sharply at her. She must try not to use words like that. People stand out a mile here just for sounding slightly different, she thought.

They were told to make their choice and that it would be ready in ten minutes. Jude ordered a ginger beer and Susie tried a sherbet drink, thinking it was a while since she'd had anything sweet. They found a quiet corner near a window and sat and watched the hustle and bustle outside. When their food was ready they ate eagerly whilst they contemplated what might be going on at home.

'It depends if we're in the same time zone,' said Jude.

'What do you mean?' Susie replied, stopping a piece of fish from falling on to her dress.

'Well… a day spent here might be only a few minutes back at home.'

'That's totally weird, kind of reassuring, but weird. How can that be possible?' Jude looked thoughtful, 'well even today time is the one element that astronomers admit they don't fully understand, but to try and simplify it, some compare it to a ride down a lazy river in a water park. Imagine you're just being carried along, not able to go any slower or faster and only stopping when you can reach for the edge.'

'I don't like the sound of that,' said Susie genuinely concerned, 'to me that sounds worryingly like being trapped in the whirl of a tornado, where there is no edge. What if you just can't get out?' Jude was about to tell her that he believed there may even be a fifth dimension of time, where there were many possible futures, but the thought of finding himself in another altogether terrified him. He calmed himself.

'Nothing that bad, I can assure you. If you miss the water's edge, you just complete the circle. Compare it to the M25, if you miss the junction you just go round again and make sure you get off it next time.' Susie loved these discussions but was well aware that Jude often went off on a tangent. She was determined to remain confident, yet the reality was that somehow they had gone back in time and there was no way she could explain it. Jude had idly wondered what he would do for a living if he had to stay here. Knowing what he did about the future gave him an unfair advantage, but he felt almost certain he would seek out the observatory in Greenwich to look at the large telescope noted for its accuracy in measuring time, and somehow be reassured.

They left the pub and turned into a narrow side street. Looking at some of the shop fronts there appeared to be workshops attached at the back where shopkeepers were able to produce their own merchandise on the premises. There were plenty of small businesses here. Glancing past windows there were only one or two people inside. The proprietor tended to be sitting near the window on high chairs next to desks that looked like glorified music stands. If you looked further into the premises the accomplice was usually sat farther away in the darker area. Small mirrors were attached to some of the windows and reflected at angles presumably to let more light into the dark buildings. Susie saw a group of children climb to the height of a well-dressed gentleman and tip his hat off, and letting it rest on his nose and then run off laughing. This was the most fun she had seen children having since she arrived, apart from the few wealthier ones she saw in Vauxhall Gardens.

'I'd like to see how the well-off live for a change, wouldn't you?'

'Of course,' said Jude, 'at the moment it seems like we're only seeing people surviving day to day, trying to avoid poverty; I suppose they are just making the best of it. But I've never seen so many entrepreneurs – people seem to have a go at almost anything.' Susie agreed and they scanned the scene. It was a difficult life. The majority of people were carrying around their livelihood on their backs or in baskets above their heads. Jude still found it hard to adjust to hundreds of people milling around, selling whatever they could and seeing animals, mainly cows, sheep and pigs, walking amongst them. He particularly noticed how many people were disabled, but there was certainly a lot of altruism here, often from children no doubt hoping for a penny or two in return. He had seen it in pubs, too, kindly looking groups of women taking people outside and offering them soft drinks from their own stands to try to sober them up.

They were back on the main thoroughfare where they saw a green omnibus with a sign saying *Tottenham Court Road* and were standing indecisively on the pavement as it meandered slowly towards them. The conductor jumped off and turned to Susie saying 'please take a seat on the bus,' as he man-handled her towards the ladder. Jude followed quickly, gathering her skirts to make it easier for her to climb on. There were no bus stops here and the driver and conductor were actively poaching people to get on all the way. The driver was well-dressed with a brightly coloured cravat, dark-grey coat and shiny boots. The conductor was more casually dressed.

'He doesn't stop shouting, does he?' said Jude, trying to block out the cries of place names to most people in the street. The bus jostled and bumped along. 'At least this is better than walking, watch out for the parasols,' he shouted to Susie above the racket. He could see people digging them into passengers near Susie with all the commotion of getting on and off. It was evident how many more women and children were travelling at this time of day, probably on days out. The bus was now in Fleet Street.

'Just look at this street,' said Susie amazed, 'it's unrecognisable apart from that church.'

'It must be the church of St. Mary le Strand that we went into on our last day trip, do you remember?' replied Jude.

'Only just – everything feels out of context.'

'I know, I keep thinking it would be great if the rest of the class were here to see all this and we could all compare notes,' he said. The bus was stopping and starting and grinding along the street. It had paused a while outside a very large building. Susie tugged at Jude's arm.

'Listen, can you hear lions?'

Jude could definitely hear roaring above the general street noise.

'It's coming from the top of that shopping arcade,' he said, incredulously.

'Don't tell me they're selling them, or maybe they're here for entertainment?'

'Dunno, I can't understand it,' Jude replied, disgusted. They were glad when the bus continued on and sat silently for a while. Susie glimpsed down Old Drury Lane and could see a cobbled road with larger paving slabs near the buildings. People were sitting on the kerbside outside a building which had double windows on either side with a big oval sign in the middle of it. It had a cockerel on it, and said '*celebrated stouts and old ales*'. She found it strange that some things were so different and yet others had hardly changed in a hundred years. She sat looking at the other passengers as the bus shuffled on until they were finally nearing the Strand and Jude suggested they get off. He leant forward and pulled gently at the conductor's coat tail, as he had seen other passengers do. It worked and they disembarked amongst a rabble of other people getting on. It was a relief to be back in the Strand. It was now mid-afternoon and they misguidedly sidled down one of the many dingy side streets. There were hundreds of pawnbrokers in this area set amongst some tiny shops selling oddities, but they both began to feel unsafe and wondered whether people coming away with money having exchanged their goods were hot targets. There were some unsavoury characters lurking around and both were keen to avoid getting mixed up in anything. Susie suggested it first, but Jude didn't need much persuading.

'Whatever happens, I think we should go back home tomorrow,' she said.

'Yes, I know, I feel the same,' he replied. Still they went in and exchanged the telephone charm without any fuss.

Back on the main street they felt instantly better and there was a buzz in the air. Entertainers were dotted around; jugglers and men and women on stilts, the women's dresses hitched up and bloomers showing. People were dressed in bright colours; terracotta, green, yellow and cornflower blue really stood out.

Susie pointed to a bustling coffee house. It was called the Cigar Divan and was a shilling to enter. It was like a lounge inside and they served coffee and sugar here. There were newspapers sprawled on a large table near the wall, and most people were chatting in small groups, reading or playing chess. They found a small table near the newspapers and Jude surprised Susie by returning with a type of lemon cordial and fruit cake. He also had a couple of small oranges in his pockets as he couldn't carry it all in his hands.

Susie went to the newspaper table and rummaged through, digging deep and pulling out a magazine from the bottom of a pile.

'Here's a copy of *Household Words*,' she said.

'Really? I've got to see this,' said Jude and leaned over to take a look. Susie couldn't help her excitement. It was hard work trying to get hold of something authentic like this for their assignments and here it was in their laps. She was aware that Charles Dickens also edited weekly magazines; and to think he could be wandering around here somewhere, she thought, feverishly skimming over the page.

'Blimey – it's *Bleak House*!' she said a bit too loudly. They started reading. 'These were the printed instalments before he got the book published,' she explained in a more hushed tone.

'Are you sure?' asked Jude. He was none the wiser. He wasn't that familiar with Dickens' work, but didn't want to start a heated argument when he could see Susie was so fired up. He left her alone to read and wandered over to the table, picking up a copy of *Bell's Life*. Flicking through he saw lots of advertisements and dotted around were the odd notices of sporting fixtures, one of which read:

'*There took place a match of football at the grounds of the White Hart on Thursday last between 12 men in the A and 12 men in the B team. After much of a wrangle, the B team prevailed.*'

So football was being played, he thought, long before the Saturday afternoon fixtures. He folded the paper and sat happily in silence for a long while. Eventually he began to focus on the people in the coffee house. There was a general restlessness about them, and many were leaving as though they were in a hurry to be somewhere else. Looking out of the window he could see a haze appearing outside. He looked at his watch, it was seven o'clock. He looked at Susie, still engrossed in the magazine, but yawning.

'I don't want to worry you,' he said, clearly alarmed, 'but it looks very murky outside.' He was stretching his neck upwards to get a better view out of the window. 'There seems to be a yellowy-green fog coming down – I think we should forget about having an evening here and try to get back to our lodgings.'

'What, after all that effort getting here?' Susie replied, still reading, but then took a look for herself. She gulped, 'that came down a bit quickly, but why don't we find somewhere to stay around here?'

'Ok, yes, that's a better idea, let's go,' said Jude.

Outside dampness had attached itself to the air, accompanied by a dense fog which must have descended very quickly. It was now a bottle-green colour and had tiny black sooty particles floating about in it. People around them were scurrying and some were holding scarves or bits of cloth over their faces to avoid breathing it in. They had been walking close to each other for about ten minutes and Susie had just linked arms with Jude when their arms were unexpectedly yanked apart. Jude was being pushed by some lads into a small street but it was impossible to see where they went in the thick haze. Frightened, Susie began to panic. She started yelling 'Jude, Jude, JUDE,' but it was hopeless, there was nothing but complete blackness and nobody was taking any notice. All she could see were pairs of legs and none of them belonged to Jude. She tried to follow in the direction he had gone, but after a while realised she was just wandering aimlessly. She called out again, but nothing. Fear gripped her but she carried on walking slowly, keeping to the edge of buildings, lit by dull yellow glows.

Eventually she found she was in Trafalgar Square. She knew because she recognised the National Gallery. From here she was looking at a large monumental lion positioned in the middle of an enormous house. She wasn't familiar with the building at all. The fog here had cleared slightly but had left an eeriness that she couldn't describe. Then she saw another familiar sight; Nelson's Column. She stared up at it and then down at the base, noticing that the lions weren't there. She stepped to one side and could see a sign saying *Charing Cross Barracks* and a group of soldiers in uniform were standing around. Not far away were a group of women, talking amongst themselves but taking it in turns to look at the men. Pretty obvious what they're here for, she thought, thinking back to the women who had grabbed Jude yesterday. Oh, Jude, where are you? she said to herself.

Then she noticed someone in a doorway staring at her. His gaze was friendly and he looked tall, thick set and was dressed like a businessman. She felt desperate to talk to someone but walked slowly passed him. In an instant he had left the doorway and was touching her elbow, 'Will you walk with me?' he asked, slightly unsure. 'Of course,' she said, glad of the company as she was frightened and lonely.

They walked slowly together for a while and at first he was very quiet, but then began a conversation.

'What is your name?' he asked.

'Susanna,' she replied, knowing by now that using the shortened version attracted too much attention.

'Well, nice to meet you Savannah.' He hadn't heard her name properly, or maybe it's too uncommon she thought. She noticed he was quite attractive, he wore a stiff white cravat and his brown hair fell around his collar and he had sideburns and a set jaw.

'What is yours?' she replied curiously.

'Hmm.' She assumed he hadn't heard her properly; he did seem a bit distracted.

'What do you do?' she asked.

'Oh, I'm a manufacturer, of furniture,' he replied. 'It's a thick fog tonight, what was your intended journey?'

'I've lost my cousin,' she blurted, clearly tearful, 'we were walking beside each other one minute and then he just disappeared.' She described Jude's build and the man said he thought he had seen a scuffle back in one of the alleyways.

'We can go and have a look if it helps,' he suggested and Susie hastily agreed. He walked quite quickly now and she stayed close, keeping to his pace. She had no idea if this was the direction she had come or not. There were people lolling around in the street, some obviously drunk, but it was still hard to see much and the atmospheric conditions had altered the street noise. She could hear a musician playing softly in the background and was surprised that he wasn't fazed by the fog, but then realised that it was only her that wasn't used to it. The man she was with unexpectedly made an abrupt turn into a quieter street and stopped at a doorway. Susie thought he was asking a potential witness about Jude but then saw him hand something to a woman who was holding a child in the hallway. That could be his wife, she thought.

They moved into a small room that looked like someone's bedroom. Within seconds he was kissing her. At first she was confused, then, feeling desperately emotional she began to kiss him back, but then quickly snapped out of it as the gravity of the situation dawned on her. This wasn't typical behaviour within minutes of meeting someone and she realised that the lady in the corridor must have been taking money for hiring out the room. He sat on the bed and tapped the space next to him for her to sit down. She wasn't sure what to do, so she sat.

'What's wrong?' he said.

'I don't even know you,' she replied. He looked astonished at this.

'But you said you'd walk with me, what is this?' he said angrily and pushed her down on to the bed. By now she could feel all his weight and alarm bells were ringing in her head. He tried to kiss her again but she contorted her body to evade him. His boot was holding her left ankle down.

'Get off me!' she shouted, but he was taking no notice. There was a loud bang outside. Startled, he looked up and Susie took the opportunity to push him off and slid out from underneath in a flash. She ran to the door and out as fast as she could and hid herself in the fog amongst the strangers. She felt lost and unbelievably lonely as tears rolled down her cheeks.

Not sure where to go she just wandered, keeping as near to the candlelit windows and gas lamps as she could. A deep tiredness came over her. She felt wretched that she had lost Jude and was angry at herself for being taken in by a stranger. It wasn't actually his fault; it was just the way things were. It seemed that most women were free and easy, despite class and despite status, but more alarming was that they all appeared content with the status quo. Yesterday she had seen a middle class woman with a ring on her finger walk off with an obvious stranger; an inherent type of behaviour for many people it seemed. Susie had assumed the woman was waiting for someone, but it was obvious now that she was a courtesan.

She wandered aimlessly, her thoughts becoming more erratic until she eventually entered a park, immediately recognising it as St. James'. She walked over a small bridge and stared down at the water. A couple of swans were nestling together at the water's edge. She stood mesmerised by the ripples in the water, her thoughts miles away. She thought of home and her family and how foolish she was being – what on earth was she doing here? Sounds of chatter and muffled laughter followed by lewd noises that she had become accustomed to, brought her back to the present moment. Continuing over the bridge and further into the park she could see a group of women lying down in a heap under one of the trees, apparently bedding down for the night. That's what I'll do, she said to herself. I can't keep going any more – I'll just stay here and sleep out in the open. She lay down practically next to the women to look as though she was part of their group. They barely seemed to notice. The fog had become thinner over the water but was dense again now. She thought about Jude and what might have happened to him and went over and over all the possible scenarios, trying not to dwell on the worst. Then her mind drifted to the history of this park. No matter how it delighted in its beauty and peacefulness during the day, with its swans, pelicans and ornamental lake, the tainted characteristic of its people seemed to penetrate the park like mould in bread. Exhaustion swept over her and within minutes she was asleep.

CHAPTER EIGHT

Jude slowly opened his eyes. When he moved he felt a slight twinge in his neck, but otherwise he felt his normal self. From what he remembered, a gang of boys had whisked him into a side street and tried to wrap a rag around his neck, twisting and pulling it. He found he had more strength than he knew and grasped the lad holding on to the rag and twisted him around to the side, slamming him on to the ground. Startled, the others joined forces, pushed him over, ransacked his pockets and then ran off quickly, leaving him bruised but sound. He sat up and checked all his pockets. He instantly noticed that his watch had gone. Now he had no way of telling the time; he couldn't even rely on Big Ben, it appeared to be missing and the tower was just a stump. He took his right boot off and shook it out and thankfully the few coins he had were still there. He felt inside his left sock and there remained his £1 coin. He decided to leave it there but put the other coins back in his inside jacket pocket. But then he froze and a wave of panic came over him; where was Susie? He got up quickly and tried to retrace his steps but the fog was still thick. He began calling her name over and over but it was like shouting into a dark abyss. Then he recognised a familiar dining house and from there he stayed close to the dim lamps and tried to make his way back to Holborn via landmarks that he recognised. But before long his bruises began to throb and he was aware of a faint headache. He felt dejected and the long walk in the hopeless fog tired him completely, so he gave up about half way and simply slid down against the wall of a building still warm from the coal embers inside. He sat still trying to remain awake, picturing Susie pacing up and down, but eventually slid into a deep slumber.

A few hours later he became aware of the low hum of street noise which, as it grew to a crescendo, eventually woke him fully and he slowly got up and stretched. He felt immediate relief that the fog had given way to a clear morning and he made his way back to their rented room. He really hoped Susie would do the same but was mindful that her sense of direction was not as accurate as his. His pace was slow but he finally approached the familiar glove shop and nearby restaurant and brushed himself down in anticipation of seeing her again. Opening the door he went straight into the hallway; there was never any talk of keys and seeing their room on the left, quickly ran in. But he was stunned to see a young man who looked to be asleep on the floor with a small trunk positioned next to him. Jude tried to register what he was seeing; looking round the room he saw that it was virtually the same as they had left it, apart from this intruder. In an instant the landlady was at the door pulling him back gently by his elbow until they were near the entrance of the house.

'What are you doing young man?' she asked.

'This is our room, what's he doing in there? We got lost last night in the fog and I can't find my cousin. Have you seen her?'

The landlady could hear the panic rising in his voice, but didn't have time for it.

'This isn't your room any more, and no she hasn't been here. If lodgers don't make use of the room it's up to them, I'm not turning away business.'

Jude could feel anger rising in his chest.

'That's not fair, we've paid for the full week, I want my money back–' but he felt defeated and trailed off as she stubbornly marched towards the front door and held it open for him. 'You need to soften your temper lad,' she said as he skulked past her, but he had sensed a tone of regret in her voice. As he wandered off he was aware that his stomach was churning and groaning. Unsure where to go next he sat down on the kerb and counted his coins. There were a few pennies there, so he walked a short way to Gray's Inn and found a popular looking coffee house. Inside it was heaving with porters and labourers and all kinds of chops, kidneys, bread and pickles were being bandied about. Without feeling inconspicuous and welcoming the distraction of watching the social hubbub, he stayed for a couple of hours. He recalled how Susie had the ability to keep him in check during his outbursts and knew he had to be more careful now that he was alone. He thought about their friendship at home. He had often turned up at her house when he was at a loose end and she had always included him in whatever they were doing. He supposed in a way she had always looked out for him. He had eaten a little and felt revived so he went back outside. Without any coherent strategy he continued strolling and found himself walking through the Seven Dials district and into Monmouth Street.

There seemed to be thousands of street vendors here, it was unbelievably busy. Men and women walked to and fro with advertising boards and in between these, static traders sold old clothes and toys. Amongst these was an elderly seller of haberdashery. For some reason Jude felt the urge to buy some ribbons for Susie, as if to reaffirm that he would be seeing her again. He bought three in different colours and handed over a penny to the grateful old man. Further along were more vendors moving around between the crowds. Everyone seemed to be calling out their wares. They were selling everything from flowers, ballads, stationery, brooms, animal food, fruit and pies to footstools, kitchen implements, coconuts, dates and dog collars. It was very lively, but again there was an underlying aggressive and desperate feel about the place. Before long he realised he was in a slum area and began noticing all sorts of shady looking characters, in particular groups of boys who had gathered erratically, clearly sizing up their victims. Jude decided to pick up his pace and try to get out of this area; he had had enough of these kinds of people. In his haste he stumbled into a street vendor's stall, nearly knocking it over. 'Oi, watch it, Hobnail!' the man cried and Jude muttered 'sorry', wondering what on earth he had meant.

From here the crowds thinned slightly and he found himself turning into Tottenham Court Road. Half way down on a corner there was a public house and in its yard he could see a large number of people gathering into what looked like teams. He crossed over and went round the side and joined them, he couldn't resist it, he assumed they were there to play football and he was eager to have a kick around, so he melted into the crowd and became part of the headcount.

'Right, we've got twenty-five on each side,' barked the man who appeared to be organising it. A few small quarrels took place about the fairness of the teams, and then someone hollered 'get ready, start' and the game began. Jude quickly threw his jacket off and ran alongside others in his group and as soon as he spotted the ball he ran towards it and smashed it over the far side, hoping one of the players would get it. The ball felt strange to him, he wasn't sure what it was made of, but it certainly didn't feel like leather. He wasn't sure why as there seemed to be an abundance of leather everywhere he went. He could see a player purposefully kicking another player's shin but the recipient just hopped and squirmed a bit and no one seemed to take any notice. As the game progressed Jude was astounded to see so many players being tripped up and hacked left, right and centre, constantly bent over double from all the pushing and shoving and digging in of elbows. It didn't take long to realise that this was indeed football but that there weren't any rules. Even worse, there didn't appear to be a goal post; nevertheless he felt invigorated and carried on ducking and diving with everybody else, until half-time.

A loud voice yelled 'all stop,' at which point Jude went over and fetched his jacket, placing it nearer to where he could keep an eye on it. He glanced around at the various players. They appeared to be of varying age, some more dishevelled than others and by the looks of it were from a mixture of backgrounds. Some had cast aside their hats, but many still wore them. But for the first time Jude noticed how happy everyone seemed to be. Despite the injuries there were smiling faces everywhere. Before long the game resumed; Jude scanned the scene to try to recognise some of his team and followed them, running backwards and forwards and even around in circles. There was no football pitch, in fact there didn't seem to be an official border line. At one point half the players went through an old ramshackle outbuilding and out the other side. The opposite team were apparently winning, so he tried even harder. His eye was on the ball and he took a giant leap towards it, barging past three other players in order to do so. At the same time someone was running towards him from his right and slide tackled him. Jude leapt into the air and fell awkwardly. Stunned for a moment, he just lay there whilst everyone else carried on playing around him. Shortly someone came and stood over him. He was blonde and looked about the same height as Jude but slightly older.

'You are alright, I take it?' he asked leaning over and offering Jude a hand getting up. 'You play quite well, kind of different. Do you always hit the ball that hard?'

'Just habit,' replied Jude.

'Well, keep it up,' said the lad, 'Calvin by the way.'

'Oh, I'm Jude.'

The game continued for a while, but Jude felt winded and took it slowly. He watched the ball but didn't make a play for it and when the game ended his team had lost spectacularly.

Not knowing which team he had even been playing for, he felt little empathy and picked up his jacket and began to walk off. Calvin caught up with him.

'Are you coming into the public house for some refreshment, it's a way of repaying the landlord for giving up his yard for us,' he said breathlessly.

'You bet,' agreed Jude, keen for a drink and some conversation.

'You bet? Bet what?'

'Just a word we use in the country,' said Jude suddenly embarrassed; he didn't want to lose the first friend he had found by saying all the wrong things. Most of the other players had the same idea and the pub soon became crowded and raucous. On the way in Calvin stopped to talk to the others and Jude decided to sneak to the far end of the bar and buy himself a drink. He was worried that he couldn't afford to buy a round and risk being caught short. Calvin had also bought himself a drink and eventually joined Jude again, not wanting to be inhospitable to a newcomer. He said he was a student and a regular player of football and wasn't short of money as his parents also lived in London and gave him a regular small income.

'So, do you live near here?' he asked Jude.

Jude sipped his ale and felt more relaxed so decided to be as truthful as possible.

'I came to London with my cousin – we were looking for jobs, we were told that this is where everyone comes to make their fortune. Yesterday evening during the fog I was robbed and I think they tried to strangle me with a scarf – they took my watch and most of my money. Now I've lost Susanna.'

'Susanna?' said Calvin surprised.

'My cousin,' explained Jude.

'Oh,' replied Calvin, 'garotted by a toy-getter,' he added pensively.

'Er, yeah,' Jude was definitely struggling with some of the jargon.

'Well, you've had a rough time of it. You can stay at mine tonight if you would like,' declared Calvin, 'I've got a suite of chambers in Grosvenor.'

Wow, thought Jude,

'If you're sure,' he said gratefully.

'Of course, and this evening we'll change and go to the Gentlemen's Club I belong to. I have supper there most evenings.'

They joined some of the other players for a second drink and then departed. Calvin flagged down a taxi who took them to the Grosvenor area. Jude was very grateful to tag along and not have to make continual decisions about his next move for a while and when they arrived at the chambers, he couldn't believe his luck. They climbed the row of steps placed between too wide pillars and a servant opened the door. They stepped into a smart hallway with shiny floorboards and a large potted fern stood near the stairway.

'Afternoon Lily,' said Calvin, 'this is Jude who will be staying here tonight.'

'Righto, sir,' replied Lily, who was a short, bubbly girl in her mid-twenties by the look of it. Her dark hair was hidden in a hair net type of bonnet and she was wearing layers of lace over a bottle-green dress. Calvin showed Jude around, pointing out the kitchen and cellars and Lily's room, and then on to the next floor where there were two sitting rooms, one with a table and chairs, which Calvin pointed out was where Jude should have breakfast at around nine o'clock, and on to Calvin's room which was quite impressive with a wooden bedstead in the centre and a large window to the front, making the room light and airy. In front of it stood a small bureau with expensive trinkets laid out on the upper shelf and clothes for the evening were laid out over a chair. Finally Jude was shown the bachelor suite at the top floor where he was to be staying. It was a neat room with a single bed, what luxury! And even a bowl with a jug of water set beside it; something he hadn't seen since he had arrived.

'If those are the only clothes you have, you'll need another evening jacket to be allowed into the Gentlemen's Club. I'll ask Lily to bring you one of mine up and we can go around five o'clock,' said Calvin.

'Perfect, I'll see you downstairs in a while,' replied Jude. He realised he needed a bit of time to gather his thoughts, it was hard work trying to think about how he formed his words and not to use slang all the time; words that simply wouldn't be understood here. He sat on the bed and had to pinch himself from lying down and staying there for two days, although the adrenaline constantly pumping would prevent that anyway. His mind went to Susie and he hoped she had enough money to find somewhere decent for the night. She was tenacious and he knew somehow that her curiosity wouldn't keep her down for too long. His subconscious mind had gone over and over ways to locate her, trying to second guess her movements, but so far nothing.

On his way down he found Calvin sitting at a large desk in the sitting room. There was also a mahogany sideboard with candelabra and silver ornaments on it and a large fireplace with two comfortable looking chairs at either side. Jude shuffled about awkwardly and then went ahead and asked casually 'Just wondering whether there is a water closet?'

'Oh, yes,' said Calvin, 'I forgot.' He pushed his chair away from the desk and pulled out the lower drawer, which was larger than the others, and pulled the two legs out which folded down. Jude stared in disbelief but had to quickly look unsurprised when Calvin glanced up at him. If this was the toilet, we may as well be camping, he thought. 'This is it, Lily takes out the slops.' Oh gross, thought Jude, who decided he would stick with the people's choice, the back garden. That's probably where the slops ended up anyway, he guessed, and into the overflowing cesspits and ultimately the wells – it didn't bear thinking about.

'Are we ready then?' asked Calvin. Jude nodded, smiling and showing no signs of despondency and felt decidedly smarter in his borrowed light brown evening jacket, and they set off.

CHAPTER NINE

Susie awoke to feel a slight chill in the air. She sat up on to her elbows, it was a cloudy day and the park was quieter, with a few people strolling and birds were flitting and swooping in the trees. She turned to her right and looked up to see the face of a cow staring down at her. Startled, she backed away, paddling with her hands until she could survey the scene fully. The group of women who had been next to her had all gone. The cow was being milked by a man sitting on a stool and there was a small queue of people waiting with vessels of different shapes and sizes in their hands. No one seemed to pay any attention to her so she sat for a while and just watched. Half way through the man took pity on her and offered her some milk from a small pan. He had probably been watching her sleep and she accepted it gratefully, giving him a timid smile in return.

Her thoughts went straight to Jude and the details of the previous night and a wave of anxiety came over her. She must go back to their room; surely he would be there waiting for her. With this in mind she jumped up and walked quickly through the park and back into the hustle and bustle of the street. She decided she would walk all the way and focused on the landmarks she knew to take her there. Wary of thieves, she erratically continued to check that her last charm and few coins were still there. Within a short distance she realised she was in Pall Mall and curiosity got the better of her when she realised the Reform Club was around here somewhere. She couldn't resist taking a look and strode purposefully for a short distance until she recognised the large building. She hesitated; this was one of the establishments of one of her idols, the French chef Alexis Soyer. She was sure that gentlemen only were allowed in, a thought that was reinforced as she observed four well-dressed men leave the building, but decided she couldn't resist a peek inside as the door was slowly closing after them. The exclusive and intimate interior was a beautifully kept square balconied area with seating high above wide square pillars. Over at the back wall she could make out a collection of art and glancing up she saw a glass domed ceiling which let in streams of light, which was effectively like looking through a kaleidoscope. She tilted her head back and twirled slowly round to magnify the effect. Then her eyes focused on a menu advertised on a door and she went towards it to take a closer look:

Soup
The Remove – *meat, game, fish*
The Entrée – *meat, sweetbreads, poultry*
First Entrements – *croquet-en-bouche, small fish, pate*
The Roast – *centrepiece*
Second Entrements – *cooked vegetables and fruit*
Dessert, cakes, pastries, macaroons, ices

Wow, thought Susie, seven courses, they eat really well here. She was hoping to see the famous lamb cutlets that she had heard was still on the menu one hundred and fifty years later, but it was not on display. She stood daydreaming for a moment when a doorman approached her and spoke softly.

'Only gentlemen allowed, madam.'

'Yes, I know – actually I was looking for Alexis Soyer–'

'Alexis resigned from here last year, madam.'

'Oh, thank you, sorry to trouble you; is he still in London?'

'I believe so, madam, now if you don't mind.'

Susie decided not to push her luck and retreated back

down the steps, welcoming the tranquillity of the area in comparison to the busy streets she was always wading through. However, she walked on, crossed Trafalgar Square and then back through the bustling Strand, gaining momentum as she tried to trace familiar steps. Before long she went through Temple Bar again, and under the cramped archway. Out the other side she noticed more vegetation and greener surroundings and feeling tempted by the smells of the street vendors she stopped to buy some hot pea soup which was served in a small delicate bowl. Her feet had begun to throb from the constant walking and she was glad to sit for a while. But the soup had not been enough; she was famished and restless, so she bought a baked apple from the next stall and ate it as she carried on with her journey.

Feeling more positive she finally came to Holborn where she paused, her heart almost missing a beat at the thought of seeing Jude again. She went straight into the hallway and turned left into their room but she could sense it was all wrong. There was no one inside but a few belongings were dotted around, including a small chest which was definitely not theirs. Overcome with sudden emotion she realised something had changed and quickly fled the room back towards the hall. She just stood for a moment, at a loss for what to do, but the landlady had heard her and asked her what she wanted.

'I thought this was our room, where's Jude, my cousin, have you seen him?' she said trying to control the tears pricking the backs of her eyes. The normally harsh woman obviously felt sorry for her and became more contrite.

'He was here looking for you,' she said sympathetically.

'When?'

'It was early this morning; I told him I hadn't seen you and that the room belongs to someone else now as I can't afford to waste it.' Susie wasn't bothered about the room she was just glad to hear he was alright.

'Do you know where he went?' she asked hopefully.

'Don't ask me, although he did mumble something about going to the West End where he felt more at home, whatever that meant,' she replied.

'Well, thank you,' said Susie who now felt a great sense of relief and joy. She still didn't know where Jude was but a least he had come looking for her. She assumed he wouldn't be coming this way again and neither would she. She decided she would splash out and take an omnibus towards the West End but disembark at Soho Square; she was more likely to find him on foot and she didn't want to miss a chance to see all the French restaurants that she knew would be here, fashioned by the influx of Frenchmen finding solace in London after the revolution; and anyway, she consoled herself, she may not pass this way again.

As soon as she arrived she was amazed at the hive of activity in the streets. For the first time she could smell fried fish and watched a few people walking about whilst eating it out of some paper. She saw a bazaar straight away and went to check it out. It was run exclusively by women who were happily going about running their own businesses. She had enquired about the price of the lace handkerchief and was told they had to cover the costs of their stalls which were 3d each to rent. It was similar to being at a car boot sale, she thought, though whether the goods were from their own homes she wasn't sure; none of it looked particularly new.

She went back out to the main road, walking slowly past some of the more interesting restaurants to read what was on the menus. She stopped at a stand where a man was claiming to be a herbalist specialising in help for dental problems and tried to decipher what on earth it was that he was wearing, it looked a bit like a dressing gown with a hood, very strange, and then across the road she saw a vendor selling ice-cream. She couldn't quite believe it, this was the first of its kind that she had seen, and knew it must be the Italian hokey-pokey so she rushed over to buy some. However she was offered a small scoop in a glass cup that she had seen the previous person lick from and to be safe she changed her mind and just stood around watching other bystanders trying to eat theirs. They obviously didn't quite know what to do with it; some were biting great chunks out of the centre and then hopping about from the pain of the cold on their teeth. Susie glanced back at the herbalist and could see the motivation for having a static stand nearby.

Feeling a little shivery partly from being around the ice-cream and partly due to the weather turning, she picked up her pace down the main thoroughfare, always on the lookout for Jude, and occasionally stopping to listen to groups of musicians and singers from around the world. There were so many distractions; a band of drummers in their colourful yellow and red traditional dress were particularly good and there were solo singers, too, wandering around with caddies for collections in their hands. She glimpsed one vocalist wandering down a residential side street singing very loudly and watched a servant run into the street and give her money, presumably to try and make her go away as she wafted her hands as if shooing a cat.

She then moved on and stood by a department store where an audience had gathered and were watching an animal act that really caught her attention too. The animal trainer had assorted animals sitting around him in a semicircle in pairs, but they were unusual pairs, pairs of animals that traditionally didn't get on. Grouped together were cats and dogs, rabbits and guinea pigs and even squirrels and hedgehogs, all sitting very still seemingly awaiting instructions. It was truly mesmerising; and the little golden cocker spaniel on the end, she thought, was gorgeous. He was just over a foot tall with alert, dark eyes but he wasn't concentrating at all on the trainer; instead he watched all the passers-by. He looked at Susie but she looked away as she didn't want to distract him any further. The animals were so amusing that she stood and watched them for a long while but then had an idea to go directly to the upmarket French restaurant called Verrey's on the corner of Regent Street. It was moments later that she realised the little cocker spaniel had followed her and was a little bit too close, sniffing around her feet. She bent down to stroke him, quietly telling him to go back, but he had already been missed. The animal trainer had spotted him walking next to her even before she had and he began yelling 'Stop, thief – stop that girl, she has stolen my dog!'

Shocked at the accusation, Susie panicked and started to run. The dog ran with her and she found herself yelling at him to go back but he took no notice, determined to be with her. She could see three men following quickly behind so she began to dart and dodge in different directions, finally hiding under a canopy. The dog didn't follow her; presumably she lost him as well and she felt immediately thankful. She could hear the men shouting and running in the distance, but the noise quickly died down and when she thought it was safe she quickly immersed herself back into the dense area of street sellers and their stalls. The incident had shaken her so much that she had forgotten where she was headed and now wanted to find somewhere warm and sociable that she could retreat to.

Further along she could see a sign for the Pantheon Bazaar and crossed the road towards it. From the outside it looked like the bazaar was set up inside an existing theatre yet was obviously now an important shopping venue judging by the sheer volume of pedestrian traffic. This was perfect but she went in cautiously, not knowing what to expect and the first thing she noticed was a sign saying '*paintings upstairs*'. She couldn't resist taking a look to see the works of the current artists. The whole area was set up in a courtyard style with pillars, iron railings and open, wide spaces. She climbed the steps to a suite of rooms above the entrance hall and wandered through to the part that housed the artwork. She could see they were mostly modern English painters and thought it was interesting that works of well-known painters were displayed for the public to see within a shopping bazaar. She started moving around the paintings, taking each one in, looking closely at some more than others. There were a few landscapes but she was more interested in the portraits. She stood in front of *The Sonnet* by William Mulready. She liked this one, a young couple in the countryside were perched on something; the girl was wearing a salmon pink dress and was covering her eyes and the lad, also in pink and peach, was tying up his shoe. Susie noticed a man move from the corner of the room towards her and was standing very close. Perhaps he was the curator, or even one of the artists. 'This is a carefree painting isn't it?' now he was by her side, eyeing her up and down as she looked at the picture, 'what do you think the girl is reading?' She looked closely and tried to guess.

'I don't know, is it a note from him?'

'Possibly, look at his face, she thinks he's adjusting his shoe, which he is, but he's also watching her, waiting for her reaction – she's covering her face but clearly laughing, it must be a joke they are sharing, possibly of a flirtatious nature.' Susie turned to look at him, wondering why he had decided to escort her around the paintings. He was an elegant man with shoulder length hair and a twinkle in his eye. He was wearing a ruffled collar, flamboyant necktie and she could smell refreshing cologne. 'And what about this one?' he said moving to a large painting at the edge of the aisle. The artist was Charles Landseer. They were looking at a woman dressed in a white lacy dress. She had an anxious expression on her face and a small brown and white dog was beside her. The gentleman began to explain.

'This, you see, depicts a forlorn woman; she has lost her lover and the dog at her side symbolises him.' Susie froze for a moment, and then glanced up at him and their eyes locked together momentarily – it's as if he knows I've lost Jude, she thought. She politely thanked him, saying she was in a hurry and backed away. He grasped her hand.

'Will you come to the Argyll Rooms tonight?' She glared at him; she had heard of the famous Argyll Rooms, a notorious pick up venue masquerading as a dance. Her reaction was instant.

'No, definitely not.' She wondered whether there was something in the Victorian air that made people relentlessly amorous. He was certainly charismatic, but she decided he was merely talking to unescorted women, probably giving them all the same spiel. Realising she was better off downstairs, she walked towards the balcony and leant against the ornamental square edging and leaned over to look down. It was positively heaving down there. Looking up at the glass ceiling, she felt like she was in a large glass aviary. The extravagance of the building was breathtaking, but it was almost eerie up here among these quiet stalls with their expensive picture frames, so she left the small art gallery, set out as though in a maze, and ventured back downstairs where the smell of exotic scents drifted through the air.

She joined the throng of people all moving in one direction past small shops selling perfumes, lace and ribbons. She noticed that it was only men serving and oddly they looked more refined and patient than the women she'd seen serving in most other shops. Further inwards, away from the shops, was a maze of stalls giving that old market feel that was evident everywhere you went. The first stall on her left was selling unusual items made of papier mâché, mostly table decorations, many of them black, but with strikingly elaborate patterns painted on. She picked something up that looked like a tray with delicate fanned edging. Seeing her confused expression, the stallholder said it was a dustpan for table crumbs but with the brush missing. The next stall simply had dolls dresses, in all sizes, and all perfectly detailed. The adjacent stall sold old flowers made from wax and the same pattern continued; most stalls were selling similar things and there was not much for men to look at either, she noticed. It reminded her of a holiday resort in Italy that her parents took her and her younger sister to, with row upon row of shoe shops, handbag shops and ice-cream parlours and practically nothing else. She was jolted back to the present by the person behind who was pushing so hard it made Susie grit her teeth but obligingly continued to move with the never-ending flow of traffic until finally it thinned; it had become impossible to stop and look properly anyway, then right at the back she could see a conservatory in the shape of a horseshoe.

This was a pleasant diversion for any weary shopper, she thought. She felt drained and reasoned with herself as to why she would want to buy anything here anyway. She suddenly felt very alone. There was a large fountain in the centre with seats around it and she quickly sat down. Dotted around were parrots and other exotic birds that were allowed to fly around freely; they were all quite noisy and chatty. Exotic palms were also placed around the edges and the light shone through the windows, making it feel really warm. There was an adjacent room for people awaiting carriages, which pulled up outside almost constantly. Posters advertised concerts that played every Thursday, which was today by her reckoning; so she slumped back and thought she would wait for it to start.

She sat as if in a trance watching people come and go and listened to them making small talk, discussing the weather and making arrangements for five o'clock tea the following week. In the background she could hear the sounds of instruments warming up above the chatter, which was becoming louder.

There was a sense of anticipation in the air like that of an audience waiting for a play to begin and then a voice suddenly boomed, 'Savannah, what are you doing here?' Susie jumped up, startled, and was about to explain, excited to distraction that somebody had recognised her – but it was a man walking towards a woman a few seats away from her. She watched the woman hold up her hand, delighted to see him and he in return grasp both of hers and sit down next to her. Disappointed and embarrassed, Susie inwardly cringed and thought she must be getting slightly delusional, who did she think she was going to see? And since when did she answer to Savannah? She needed fresh air and remembering where she was previously headed, went straight out in the direction of Regent Street.

CHAPTER TEN

She stopped to ask the time, choosing a well-dressed gentleman who looked as if he owned his watch, and not stolen it. 'Four o'clock, madam,' was the reply. She thanked him and looked around; there were some interesting shops on Regent Street; one clothes merchant appeared to own nos. 114-120, each window advocating different types of dress. She idled past, intent only on window shopping. One window displayed material and designs, presumably to tell the public that they manufactured on the premises, the next was devoted to uniforms for diplomats and the military, after that there were colourful robes and costumes and the last window advertised clothing for boys. The buildings on this street seemed very grand and interspersed between them were smaller individual shops, one of which was selling expensive soap. Soap, she thought dreamily and pictured herself in a bath filled to the top with bubbles; so far she hadn't met many people who seemed to know it existed. She stood nearer to take a look at the prices and then realised why. The yellow and white cleansing household soap was 7 shillings and the Spermaceti navy soap for sea water was 8d. The toilet soaps weren't much better, turtle oil soap was 2s and 6d and the Chinese soap was even more expensive. She presumed these were taxed highly; no wonder the poor didn't bother getting washed around here, soap was out of their financial reach.

The air was chilly and the street steadily became less busy; she could hear the sound of her boots clonking on the damp pavement as if to remind her of how alone she really was. A panicky feeling came over her as her adrenalin rose, an urgent feeling that she needed to get off the street, and she was reassured when she finally walked up to the corner of Hanover Street and saw the welcoming Verrey's restaurant, all lit up. Almost tiptoeing she looked through the windows and saw waiters busy laying the tables for the evening ahead; the interior looked ornate and stylish with three chandeliers hanging in the centre of the room. She went towards a menu attached to the door and scanned it – *Petite marmite, Potage à la Verrey , Oefs à la Russe, Soufflé de filets de sole, Noisettes d'agneau à la Princesse, Pommes Mirelle*; it all sounded extravagant, she thought, but couldn't really understand any of it.

There was a lot of noise coming from the kitchen below and out of curiosity she walked down the steps and stood in the doorway which was left wide open. Clouds of steam came from large pots bubbling in different areas and the room felt welcoming and warm. The head chef was giving orders in a thick French accent and the staff busily followed them. She gazed at the layout of the kitchen. High racks housed pots and pans and lids were hung up separately, furniture resembling dark wooden wardrobes contained earthenware dishes and plates and utensils hung from pillars in the centre of the room. The cooks looked like they were wearing sailors' hats and the atmosphere appeared orderly and chaotic at the same time. She had hoped there was a small chance that the head chef would be wearing a beret and, disappointed that it wasn't him, turned to walk away, but he suddenly turned round and noticed her.

'Ah, there you are ma Cherie, you are late, but no matter – over here please.' He threw her a large white apron and, completely taken aback, she automatically put it on. She had no idea what was going on; although it was obvious she had been mistaken for somebody else but she didn't really care, she was eager to do something. He looked over her shoulder towards the yard.

'Your dog is not allowed in here.'

'Oh, you are mistaken, I–'

Susie followed the chef's unfaltering gaze and realised that the cute golden spaniel that was part of the troupe had followed her here.

'He's fine,' she replied more confidently than she felt, 'he's no trouble, he always stays outside until I have finished.'

The chef had no time for this and just shrugged and continued.

'I want you to work on the sauces.' He pointed to an empty work station, 'here – you know what to do, eh?' He could see Susie looked hesitant, 'Ah, but you are new here, I will show you.' He went on to concoct a sauce that began with onions and mushrooms, adding drops of condiments, some from bottles without labels. He worked quickly and she tried not to miss a thing.

'Et voilà! this is your basic sauce and then you substitute one of these special ingredients when the different orders arrive.' She tried to keep up as he reeled off the herbs and spices and nodded to show she had comprehended. The finished sauce looked shiny and smelt delicious; she was sure she could do it but she couldn't bring herself to start. The chef had noticed and was becoming abrupt and uptight.

'You are here for the evening to make sauces, yes?'

'Yes, that's right,' she said, 'I'll start straight away.'

'Very good,' said the chef and walked away. She could see the yard from there and sensed the dog felt more comfortable knowing that he could still see her. He tilted his head slightly, his tail wagging, then, satisfied he could see her went and sat by the bins. Looking around the kitchen most of the staff were men, apart from a girl doing the washing up over at the far side and another near her who was preparing vegetables. She could hear the French chef explaining to his soux chef that Susie must have been sent in place of Henrí, his hands and eyebrows were raised, but then everybody just carried on, too busy to care. She found the basic sauce recipe, stained but readable and feeling fairly confident got stuck in.

For brown sauce to accompany meat: use chopped onion, add chilli vinegar, then common vinegar, colouring, water, mushroom ketchup, anchovy. She had put all of these in a pan and then set it on fire, like the recipe suggested. Melted butter.... surely that was straightforward. She hesitated and glanced around the kitchen uncertainly. The vegetable girl had seen her indecision and was soon by her side.

'You look bewildered.'

'Yes, I'm not sure what this means.' She read *melted butter* aloud. 'It is just butter melted isn't it?' she suggested carefully.

'How can you be a cook if you don't know this?' replied the girl who began to demonstrate, 'you put butter and flour together with salt and pepper, mix it, and add one pint of cold water, warm it and then add more butter.' She handed the spoon back to Susie, 'now mix with your brown sauce.'

'Of course, of course, it's called something else where I am from, that's all – thank you.'

The girl shrugged and went back to her vegetables. Susie was relieved but was starting to lose confidence. She watched the vegetable girl for a while. It certainly looked like intricate work. She was thinly slicing a mix of vegetables into disc shapes and making a tower out of them. On a separate plate she had arranged peas, beans, truffles, potatoes and beetroot into a mosaic pattern, waited for another chef to place some saucisson on top, and then dressed the whole thing with whipped egg whites. Impressed at the delicacy, Susie continued to make the other sauces with vivacity, no longer questioning unusual combinations such as something that resembled yellow chutney combined with vinegar to accompany fish.

She had been working constantly on the sauces and came

to a natural break. She had prepared a substantial amount and had hardly looked up when she suddenly remembered the dog; he was still there. She checked that no one was looking and snatched a bone from a discarded pile and tossed it towards him and he began gnawing on it immediately. On her way back she saw another chef flambé an omelette with rum and pass it to a waiter for immediate dispatch.

'Come now,' said the chef to everyone, 'we eat quickly before the rush.' Everyone sat down wherever they could and quickly and precisely ate the food that was put in front of them. To Susie's amazement it was the same food that she had read on the menu and the parmesan coated sole in particular tasted delightful to her. She was also excited to try Verrey's own special coffee which she knew was amongst the most celebrated in town. Everyone clearly enjoyed the food but there was no time for chat which she was grateful for as her mind was too preoccupied to answer any personal questions. She soon went back to her sauces for four more hours after which time she was feeling far more confident. Her adrenalin was still high when the chef appeared by her side to address the staff in a precise manner.

'That is all for tonight, the service is coming to an end, thank you for your efforts – we will see you tomorrow night, eh?' He placed some money in Susie's hand. She smiled awkwardly as she wasn't expecting to be paid there and then, never mind coming back tomorrow, but then wondered what else she would do if she hadn't found Jude; maybe she would return, even if it was just to sample another of those dinners.

The dog wasn't there this time and she wasn't sure whether to be relieved or sad. Coming out of the door behind her were the chefs she had been working with. They were chatting excitably and one of them tapped her gently on the shoulder asking her to join them.

'Where are you going?' she said.

'To a supper house of course,' said one of the chefs in a French accent. The others were a mix of French and British.

'Well alright, but can we stop by Oxford Street first, I need to find somewhere to lodge.'

'What, you don't have anywhere to stay?' said one of the chefs, alarmed.

'No, I'm new here.'

'Yes, we can do that—' said the girl, looking round at the others who nodded their consent as it was only a short distance to Oxford Street.

Despite the three chefs and the vegetable girl knowing each other well, they were very friendly and obliging towards Susie and escorted her to sleepy Oxford Street with its small hotels dotted in amongst the shops. Not wanting to waste time she stopped at the first suitable place which resembled something between a small private hotel and lodgings.

'Here will do,' she said, 'I'll just be a minute.' The others hung around outside laughing and joking to themselves whilst she secured a room. Inside she was told there was only one single room that was vacant and that it was 4d a night with breakfast provided. She handed over the money there and then just to secure it. When she emerged outside again she realised that she still hadn't had a proper introduction, but it wasn't forthcoming and somehow it didn't matter. Their carefree attitude had rubbed off on her and she was just glad to be out socialising. One of them told her that the supper house was in the piazza in Covent Garden. It didn't take long to get there as they seemed to know all the short cuts and the route they took was littered with lively night spots. She felt much safer in the dark being with locals and it was great to see London at night. The animals were silent and the cacophony on the streets had quietened down. She could hear music coming from intimate bars and lounges and as they brushed by the edge of the Haymarket the night scenes were gaudier and racier. They passed Tavern dancing rooms and she guessed by the atmosphere that this was the infamous brothel hotspot. Davy had told them there were around one hundred and eighty in this small area alone. Now she could see it for herself; women were flaunting themselves in the streets and as she peered into one of the accommodation houses she could actually see men and women openly negotiating and handing over money.

Once in Covent Garden they descended some stairs and a waiter stood with the door open to let them in. The first thing that hit her was the smell of smoke and clouds hung thick with it in the air, but the atmosphere was intoxicating. The venue was large enough to hold a thousand people and the girl told her that the clientele was a mixture of businessmen, country gentlemen, army officers and students. They were shown a seat upstairs as men only were allowed on the ground floor, but they were given a large table overlooking the stage area below.

The waiter passed them all a songbook and stood and waited. Susie flicked through and noticed that the songs were all numbered. He then offered them a choice of stout or grog and later came back with several glasses of both. When she was sure no one was looking Susie quietly asked the waiter what grog actually was.

'Why, it is lemon juice and water, sugar, cinnamon and rum of course!' he replied rather too loudly. Two of the chefs looked up from their books as if weighing her up. Flustered, she took one of the drinks and smiled gratefully, 'Oh, yes, I'd forgotten.'

Food orders were taken then and shouts of eggs, steaks and chops were given, so Susie joined in asking for poached eggs. When the food arrived around forty minutes later, it was much better quality than anything she had expected and enjoyed it while watching three men singing on the stage, accompanied by a piano player. After a short break another man leapt on to the stage dressed like a clown announcing that comic songs would be next and called out a number. All her friends were leafing through their songbooks and it reminded Susie of being in a church and the hymn number being called out. Although to her disbelief the content couldn't have been more different. The songs were unbelievably crude and at first she struggled to join in. Looking around, no one else seemed embarrassed and they all sang along with the compere. She soon found it hilarious and was bent over double laughing along with everyone else.

During an interval Ethiopian serenaders were announced who came on in their colourful costume. Susie recalled seeing them as street entertainers a few days earlier and thought then how good they were. Finally, the operatic section was announced and everyone joined in with vigour, some sitting, some standing and swaying; the atmosphere was fantastic – but all too soon the evening was coming to an end. She heard someone mention that the Covent Garden market traders would be arriving shortly and everyone in the crowd laughed even though it was actually not far from the truth.

'How do we pay?' she asked one of the chefs.

'We pay on the way out, at the door,' he replied. Susie worried slightly about the final bill, but the waiter at the door simply asked what they had had and before she could answer two of the chefs brightly said 'five glasses each of stout and grog and two poached eggs.' They paid with a few shillings and they all left. Susie didn't say anything but knew they had missed out a couple of meals; either they were too drunk to remember or had simply pulled a fast one. They were all quieter walking back; the cheery effects of all the fun they had had was wearing off and was now replaced with lethargy and an eagerness to get home. Two of the chefs turned off into a small street but the remaining chef and the girl went out of their way and accompanied Susie to the corner of Oxford

Street, where she thanked them graciously and said goodnight.

Her room was facing the street and she went straight over to the window to peer out at the view. She had had a great time, but it was such a relief to be inside and to have privacy again. She looked up towards the night sky as she processed the events of the day. Looking at the bright moon it was strange that this was the only familiarity to her. She remembered Jude telling her that in their time the moon was slowly moving away from the earth. She stared at it, was it really any nearer now? She began looking around her room and could see it was furnished sparsely but at least it had a bed. She went over and sat on it to take her boots off, then swivelled her legs round on to the bed and lay staring at the ceiling, deep in thought. Her feelings returned to Jude; she missed him so badly. She tried to picture his bright eyes and the way his hair nestled around his shirt collar – she must surely find him soon.

CHAPTER ELEVEN

'Come on,' said Calvin, 'I'll take you to Rotten Row.' Rotten Row, Jude mused, not sure that he liked the sound of it. However he couldn't have been more wrong as apparently it was part of Hyde Park nestled among trees. The weather had been dull and drizzly all day so far but now the sun was peeking through, splitting the clouds and paving the way for a pleasant evening, albeit short, until dusk. Rotten Row appeared to be the name of a long strip like a carriageway running from east to west. The end that they were approaching was busy with carriages and there was a jovial excitement amongst the passengers and drivers. There was a raised boardwalk which was thick with onlookers who stood holding on to wooden railings and Calvin and Jude joined the crowd at one end.

Looking around Jude noticed how affluent they all looked, parading around in their finest gear as though it was Royal Ascot. The real wonder, though, was the horsemanship. The parade appeared to be dominated by women riders; one in particular was well known to the crowd who cheered her on as she rode past at speed, the feather in her cap flapping backwards. The other passengers were enjoying a more sedate ride, parading up and down, smiling and nodding to the hangers-on. There was a pleasant atmosphere, and again Jude thought it brought light relief from seeing beggars in the streets trying to flog paintings and others picking out pennies from cracks in the pavements, although he had felt very sorry for them all. The harsh reality of the wide gap between the rich and the poor was obvious; it wasn't that wealthy people didn't want to help the poor; they just didn't want to be living amongst them. He was leaning over too far but before he could pull himself back one of the horses brushed past him a little too close for comfort, slamming his shoulder and knocking his hat off, which he snatched back before it touched the ground.

'Don't lean over like that you fool, you nearly lost your tile!' said Calvin.

'Yeah, I know, I need to keep my wits about me,' replied Jude rubbing his shoulder and trying not to wince.

'Your what?' asked Calvin, struggling to hear.

Realising he may have said the wrong thing Jude repeated, 'Yes, I know, got no more hats with me.' Calvin just nodded, thinking how strange Jude appeared sometimes. He just didn't seem to a have a clue about anything. Calvin had been schooled in the art of diplomacy from an early age by his parents. He always had to think before he spoke; the only activity that allowed him to be himself was when he played football. Meeting Jude had widened his perspective; he liked his spontaneity in action and in thought, although he couldn't understand why he kept using the letters O and K together. He watched the procession. They had got there rather late and it was slowly drawing to a close and the crowds started to drift away. He checked his watch, 'almost seven o'clock, I'm starving, let's go the Club.'

'Okay,' replied Jude and Calvin frowned.

They walked to the Gentlemen's Club as it was only a short distance away. From the outside it looked like a large classical style building and as expected it was very plush inside. There was a grand staircase and gallery with apartments leading off. Jude could see why these places were popular, every need seemed to be catered for and it felt very homely; no wonder they were known as second homes for men. There was a library to the left and there was a separate lounge, dining room, smoking room, coffee room and cards room. It reminded him of a glorified youth club without the chandeliers. There were servants around, all part of the annual cost, he was told. Apparently meals could be had at any time, but dinner seemed to be taken by small groups for social reasons and as it was just being served they sat down straight away.

'It's good and cheap,' said Calvin to Jude more quietly than usual. He was aware of Jude's financial circumstances, 'only 5 shillings.' Cheap, thought Jude, he must be joking, and hastily told Calvin that he'd left his money back at the chambers.

'That's not a problem, you can repay me later,' he replied patting Jude on the back.

Calvin was very familiar with the others who joined them for the meal and he trusted they would be pleasant enough to his special guest. Jude had worked out that there were four courses and he hoped there would be no awful surprises. He had an overwhelming desire for a simple cooked meal in his own home, but clear soup arrived first, to his relief and was accompanied by a drink.

'What's this?' he asked the waiter amid a few surprised glances.

'Madeira wine, sir.'

'It's what we have after soup, Jude, stop asking questions,' said Calvin slightly embarrassed.

Next it was white 'fish of the day'. Cutlery was provided and Jude automatically picked up his knife and fork, but the room went a little quiet. One of the men teased.

'What are you, a Goth? – it is silver blades for fish, not steel knives, they just go rusty.'

A few others sniggered and Jude looked decidedly uncomfortable. He watched the others wait for silver blades to be brought to them and did as they did. Calvin didn't seem to notice Jude becoming quieter as the meal progressed, but Jude needed to concentrate on observing the etiquette so as not to stand out even more. The conversation was about literature and as this was not Jude's favourite subject he just listened and observed the servants. One of them was preparing drinks over at the sideboard. He poured sherry into a jug and put lemon peel, sugar and a bunch of nettles in with it, let it sit for a few minutes, and then strained it. He then added this to some white wine and brought it over to Jude.

'Moselle cup, sir.' At least Jude didn't need to ask this time; it was almost as though the servant felt sorry for him. This was really not his style, but despite himself he was enjoying the experience. Next to arrive was a roast joint of some sort accompanied by a different wine. The conversation was getting louder and more amiable and had turned to the state of the railways. 'Sherry cobbler, sir,' said the waiter handing him a glass. Calvin again could see Jude was puzzled and whispered 'sherry, bingo and nutmeg.' If you say so, thought Jude, realising he had had so much to drink he didn't really care any more.

'I think they should get rid of third class, it's awful that the carriage doesn't even have a roof and the sides of the carriages are only half that of the other classes. Those poor passengers must perish when the weather is ghastly, and the noise—' said one diner. Jude thought he had a point and reflected on the many college discussions about the fact that although technology had grown in leaps and bounds, somehow it did so at the expense of the population. His thoughts suddenly turned into frustration and he couldn't stop the blurred words from tumbling out.

'I think it's extraordinary that feats in engineering are going on every day and yet basic sanitation needs aren't being met. What I can't understand is why it's taking you so long to figure out the dire need for sewers. Why aren't there any toilets? And there's hardly any clean water!' There were some raised eyebrows and mumblings around the table.

'Not quite right, we get water,' interrupted one of the diners.

'Yes, maybe some, a few hours a week,' said Calvin in a huff, but agreeing with Jude.

'Actually, we get water three hours a day, three times a week.'

Jude was getting more agitated, 'and you think that's enough? Don't you wonder why people get ill? Thousands of people died in the last cholera epidemic only two years ago. The spread of cholera's not miasmic like most people seem to believe, it comes from the bloody water!'

As soon as he'd said it, his hand came towards his mouth as if to shut himself up and he quickly added, 'I'm sorry, it's the wine—'

Meanwhile some jellies arrived and Jude was thankful that the dinner was coming to an end as he was feeling pretty grim. One of the other students was now going on about the poor and talking about the workhouses being the last best hope. Jude felt that it was all so one-sided and started up again.

'But it's the countrymen that are gradually being made redundant, they don't particularly want to come here, they have no choice; some of them have to rely on the monetary system for the first time. I think that's terrible, it's like every man for himself, the poor people have been badly let down, uncared for since the dissolution of the monasteries; the monks always took care of the poor.'

The room had gone quiet and tension hung in the air. Someone around the table tried to alleviate it by ignoring the whole topic of the poor and agreeing with what Calvin had said on the previous subject of the drinking water.

'Yes, there was an article in *Household Words* in March that mentions the imperfect sewers and that in effect we are all drinking the river water.' Calvin, though, had heard enough of Jude's outbursts and began fidgeting until he pushed his chair back quickly, making excuses that his friend was probably tipsy. Jude went to get up too, but the waiter announced 'oyster toast', putting a large plate down on the table. He had to try this, and so grabbed a piece, taking a bite out of it as he got up from the table, but his leg became caught in the chair which somehow tipped him over. He picked himself up off all fours as the diners looked on in amazement, but once in the foyer Calvin looked sternly at Jude.

'I'm not sure what that was all about, but you are full of fancy. You should sit in the library for a while and calm down. I'll get one of the servants to bring you some coffee from the coffee room. 'I'll be playing cards, come and join me when you feel a bit better,' he said as he started to walk off.

'Calvin I'm sorry,' Jude replied, 'it's just that I'm only used to drinking cider in the country.' Calvin paused, 'it doesn't matter, you were only defending your countrymen.'

In the library Jude felt relieved to sit quietly on his own whilst the others retired to the other rooms in the club. He drank the coffee and began to feel calmer, thinking it must have been the concoction of drinks that got him riled. He knew his points were valid, but also knew he had to be careful, remembering that people were sent to prison just for knocking on doors and running away here. He was also feeling guilty about manufacturing his past but knew there was little else he could do at present. He got up and walked around the library. Paintings in ornate frames filled the walls and books were packed horizontally and vertically into impressive bookshelves. There were vast collections including the classics and over on a circular side table were a few select books marked 'latest', one entitled *The Stones of Venice* and the other *The King of the Golden River,* both by John Ruskin and neither of which he recognised. He thought he might see *Moby Dick*, but perhaps it was too early. He went over to the unit that housed maps, newspapers and periodicals and found a small section holding newspapers from the previous few years. He picked up a copy of the *Morning Chronicle* which showed chutes from the Fleet,

Tyburn, Effra and Neckinger rivers discharging into the stream. It went on to describe Bermondsey as '*the capital of cholera*' with the passage of sewage travelling directly into the river. Jude wished he had the paper at the dinner table, but the fact that the newspapers had highlighted the impact of filth on disease at all made him think that perhaps they were all more aware of the situation than he thought. Feeling slightly vindicated for his earlier outburst at the dinner table and feeling more or less back to normal, he decided it was time to join the others.

He went to the card room and saw that the player sitting next to Calvin was leaving so he sat down in his place in time for a new game to begin. He was used to playing cards. When he was about fourteen his father had started a routine of family card games on a Friday night which they all looked forward to and Jude had a knack of remembering most of the rules of the four or five games he had learnt. Sometimes they played for sweets and other times for money, although it was always small change.

He hoped they had forgiven his outburst at the table earlier and asked them what game they were playing.

'It's Loo,' replied one of the players.

'Loo?' asked Jude, looking over at him and expecting him to burst into laughter. He thought they were getting their own back after the conversation about the toilets, but then he realised they wouldn't be familiar with the term yet and anyway they were all concentrating hard on the game.

'Lanterloo, you know,' said Calvin, 'in case you've forgotten we are each dealt five cards and you have to try to take tricks, it's free if you want to abandon your hand, but the cash stays in the middle.'

'Yes, I see,' said Jude picking up his cards, 'I'll remember quickly once I begin playing.' He was getting used to bluffing. As it happened the game was similar to poker and he had played a little of that before at least.

Everyone around the table was quite chirpy apart from Calvin who mouthed to Jude that he was losing. Jude played with pennies to begin with but as he got more confident, he started winning more than he lost, and began to win back shillings. By now Calvin had lost all his money, abandoned his hand and got up to leave the table. He slumped onto a leather sofa and sat with his feet up and arms folded. He was quite in awe of Jude's luck, though, and kept watching avidly, he had a bird's-eye view of his hand. Jude was having a lucky streak and became more nervous as he could now see sovereigns in amongst the winnings, but he knew he already had a lot of money under his belt and he eventually wrapped up his game – it wasn't the same with Calvin out of the loop.

'Come on,' said Calvin more cheerfully, 'why don't we go to the theatre?'

'Good idea,' replied Jude who was in high spirits after his huge winnings. It was amazing, a small aristocratic fortune given to him over a game of cards. He gave Calvin the money he owed for the dinner and offered to pay for the rest of the evening. They said their goodbyes and got a ride straight to the Theatre Royal on Drury Lane.

There were a few stragglers outside the theatre as most people appeared to have already arrived and were seated. Calvin hurriedly explained that *The Queen of Spades* was playing and Jude nodded excitedly, although he had never heard of it.

'Don't we need to stop here?' asked Jude hesitating outside a shop window next door that advertised quality great coats, opera glasses and bonnets for hire, as well as *'books of the opera'*. He had assumed they were going to an opera.

'It's not an opera; the Italian Opera House is over there.' Jude turned and observed the wealthy clientele going towards it. Calvin watched him staring and misreading him thought he was disappointed not to be going, so he sighed and explained, 'wealthy commoners pay 150-400 guineas for the season, but it is 6 shillings for a ticket in the pit from any local bookseller if the subscriber isn't using it. If you'd rather, we can–'

'No, no–' interrupted Jude, 'I'm not bothered at all, come on, let's go.'

Calvin sensed Jude didn't have the slightest idea where to go and steered him in the right direction.

'It's a bit late but we are allowed to go in during the Second Act for half the price,' he said pulling Jude towards the tout standing outside the theatre, before they missed too much. Once inside they hurried to their seats; the atmosphere was lively to say the least. Jude checked out his surroundings. The theatre was enormous and in front of him royal boxes overhung the forestage on both sides. The curtains were a gold colour and framed the stage like lace effect waves of icing draped over a wedding cake. Above these were magnificent engravings on the ceiling. The theatre was lit in a glow of splendour all around the edges where the audience sat. Jude and Calvin were in a row that was below the rest of the audience and Jude finally focused on the actors, who were good, and yet every now and then someone would holler something directly at them and interrupt them, making them uneasy and the play uncomfortable to watch. Some members of the audience joined in and others were incensed by it, causing the odd brief slanging match.

Jude was trying to work out the story in the play. From what he could gather it was set around a card game and the obsession of one man to find the secret card and win his fortune. But the play also had flashbacks and some lines were spoken in French and yet the play seemed to be set in Russia. It might have helped if they had seen it from the beginning; it was hopeless, but he didn't mind, it was such a novelty being able to see a play at all. He was just getting into it and watched one of the actresses speak her line.

'Oi, can't hear you, speak up!' yelled someone from the

audience, followed by uproarious laughter from others in the crowd. Continuous heckling seemed to follow and the atmosphere made Jude feel on edge. To make things worse he felt something cold and damp being thrown over him. He looked down and realised that they had both been pelleted with orange peel, but Calvin didn't appear bothered. Jude had had enough; irritated and angry he shot out of his seat and turned round yelling 'you're a bunch of hooligans, the lot of you!'

'Sit down,' said Calvin mortified, 'this happens all the time, people always throw their rubbish into the air.' Unbelievable, thought Jude, who by now was really hacked off and he thought about Susie, if he had been with her they probably would have just laughed and he suddenly felt desperate to see her again. The play finally ended and they sat waiting for the theatre to empty slowly. Calvin turned to Jude.

'What is your problem, it's as though you've never been to a big town before, is the country really that different? The cab asked for half-a-bull and you didn't know how much that was, and you say you don't know any French, you must know some – most of the menus are in French. I think perhaps you are taking me for a fool; are you from the continent?'

'No, I'm not – look I'm sorry, it really is different where I'm from but truthfully I'm distracted because I'm worried about my cousin.' Calvin could sense the sadness in Jude's voice.

'Oh yes, I forgot,' he replied, a little softer. 'I suggest we walk home and look out for her on the way.' Like that's really going to work, thought Jude, but tried to lighten up; he knew Calvin's intentions were good and right now he was the only friend he had.

Although the aim was to go straight home, turning the corner they began to blend in with hundreds of other people leaving the theatres and saloons. As soon as those establishments had closed another round of entertainment rooms had opened up. It wasn't just the main thoroughfare that had come alive, but the whole piazza. People were whistling and shouting to each other in the streets and places had become brightly lit with music streaming from most of them. Jude watched people flock excitedly into large concert halls. Some women were wearing silk dresses, others wore layers of lace, but they all looked elegant. He stopped at the entrance to glimpse inside.

'Don't be fooled by the expensive gowns, they are still mostly out to earn,' said Calvin, 'they mingle in the restaurants and assembly halls like this one.' He caught the despondent look on Jude's face.

'Don't despair; it's a way of life, it's a good time to make money, after midnight.' Jude thought it made sense. He knew about the situation for women at this time. They basically had no rights of their own. Even if they attained land and wealth, their commoner husbands could easily relieve them of both. He watched them again; this was one of the few ways for them to gain independence and he was beginning to feel sorry for them, but he was glad of the warning; some of the women were quite attractive and he didn't want to get drawn in.

They walked along until they came to smaller establishments, reminiscent of dimly lit romantic wine bars. Calvin explained that the music and jovial sounds were coming from the night houses which had kitchens and tables, some with small bands and dance floors and that some of them were probably unlicensed. The Turkish Divans with their lounges and bars were smaller but still seemed luxurious inside. Peering in Jude could see that for these people the night had only just begun. He was determined to sample the night life so he didn't hesitate to accompany Calvin into a place called Sally's.

Inside both sexes were mingling together, chatting, drinking and eating. Smoke filled the air and a small band including drummer and violinists played evocative music in the background. The scene reminded Jude of 1950s America where young and innocent couples met over ice-cream while listening to the jukebox. This scene, though, was far more discerning; there was a more urgent feel about the way the couples behaved; drink was flowing quickly and again it looked like negotiation rather than conversation. Jude bought them both a glass of rhubarb champagne for 6d each and they both propped up the bar, content just to watch. Every now and then they could hear laughter coming from the rooms above. Jude whispered to Calvin, 'you don't think we'll be propositioned do you?'

Calvin smiled at his ignorance, 'No indeed. In case you hadn't noticed the women here don't openly gaze at you and address you first; they wait to be approached – although it's not like that everywhere in London.' Yeah, I know, thought Jude, remembering his near abduction by some really rough women only a couple of days ago. He remembered their beer stained clothes and matted hair and shuddered. More people were coming in the door all the time and an hour of people watching had gone by and they ordered another glass each. Calvin seemed happy to let Jude pay and Jude felt that it wasn't really his money anyway, but was careful not to blow it all on one night. Suddenly his heart began to race. Over at the other side of the bar he thought he could see Susie. Rushing over he flung his arms around her waist and whisked her round shouting 'Susie!' He was convinced it was her and hugged her tight. The surprised woman pushed him off and stared at him; it wasn't her at all. He felt ashamed and tried to reason why she would be here in the first place, but by this time the man she was with had pulled Jude towards him by his necktie and stamped on both his feet.

'Get off me,' yelled Jude, startled and hurt, 'it was an honest mistake.'

The man let him go with a shove.

'Get your own,' he muttered and staggered off.

Jude was by now overwrought, he was furious and frightened and asked Calvin if he was ready to leave. Calvin had seen the whole incident and was staring at Jude's unusual shirt collar which was now showing, but he chose to ignore it.

'I know you are concerned for your cousin, Jude, but you waltz around in the most repulsive manner.' They walked home together hardly exchanging any words.

CHAPTER TWELVE

Jude had overslept. He couldn't remember having ever been so tired and barely remembered getting back to the chambers and his own bachelor suite. His toes were aching. He had no idea of the time but could see daylight peeking through the thick, red curtains. It was so much quieter here; he could hear a few birds in the trees, and for a flickering moment he thought he could actually be at home and sincerely wished it was so. His stomach started to turn over with hunger which brought him to his senses and he got washed in freezing cold water which made him hop around and get dressed promptly. He went through the house trying to see if anyone was at home; there didn't appear to be anyone living here other than Calvin and Lily and no doubt Calvin's parents paid a good few guineas a year for the privilege. Drawn to the sound of voices Jude found himself wandering towards the kitchen below and stood in the doorway. Lily was standing at the sink peeling vegetables, talking to a man sitting repairing the handle of a saucepan.

'He's got this strange way with words,' Lily was saying.

'Oh? How so?' asked the man.

'Well, he keeps saying 'Hi' to start with; we're not horses you know–'

Hearing this Jude entered the kitchen making sure he used a different greeting.

'Good morning.'

Lily jumped slightly when she saw him, she hadn't realised he was there. There was an awkward silence and he guessed that this wasn't his territory and that she would probably only respond if he spoke first. He knew by their mutterings that they were suspicious of him by now.

'I apologise, I think I overslept,' he said.

Lily dried her hands on her apron. 'I brought you up hot water at eight o'clock but you were out sound.' He felt a little awkward because she was about the same age as him yet acted as though she had forty years behind her. She, on the other hand, was treating him with caution; it wasn't just his conduct, she thought he looked different too. Jude thought she seemed rather bashful as she continued.

'Your breakfast was served at eight-thirty, but I took it away because it was cold in the end.' Jude felt uncomfortable that she was serving him at all. At this point the pan mender stood up saying it was as good as new, took his money and left. Jude cleared his throat; he was feeling really self-conscious now.

'I don't have the time I'm afraid; I couldn't set my alarm as I recently lost my watch.' Lily raised her eyebrows, finally in tune with what he was saying.

'Alarm? Do you mean alarum, the new idea to wake people up in the morning? There's one down at the Exhibition, it's a silent alarum bedstead which at daybreak can push the sleeper into a sitting position and then out of bed and into a cold bath; it looks a bit odd.'

'Yes, I suppose it would.'

Lily looked thoughtful, 'why don't you just ask a policeman, it's part of their job, a lot of people ask them if they're not any good at rising in the early hours. I know a few Bobbies that patrol round here; I'll ask one for you if you like.'

'No, no that's not necessary, but thank you all the same,' he said quickly; he needed to remain as inconspicuous as possible, at least until he found Susie. Lily studied him carefully, 'then again I don't suppose you need someone to wake you in the country; I imagine the cockerels do it.' She was testing him, but he was prepared.

'Actually we all go to bed early to save on fuel and candles, so naturally we get up at dawn.'

'What sort of work do you do in the fields?' She wasn't going to let it go so he took time to answer.

'When I was around six or seven years old I ran around scaring the birds for hours and hours. Then when I was older I ploughed the fields and harvested all day.'

'Oh, I see.' Lily finally changed the subject.

'I can make you an egg and some kidneys if you like.'

'Just an egg, thank you,' he replied, thinking he would almost retch if he had to eat kidneys for breakfast.

'Do you want some tea?'

'Tea – I haven't seen much of that–' he trailed off but then said loudly, 'Er, yes – thank you, I wasn't aware that you had some.' He hoped she hadn't heard the first bit as she went down the steps to the cellar. He cringed and told himself he must think before he speaks, he'd only been up a few minutes and was already in danger of making a faux pas.

It appeared that Lily had heard him say 'yes' and carried on the conversation from there. 'Calvin's mother and father always give me tea and sugar at Christmas and I try and make it last the year.'

He watched her make it and thought that this cosy kitchen was the nearest he had felt to being at home yet. She put the tea down before him; he had forgotten what a refreshing drink it was, his egg came soon after that and Lily carried on with the vegetables while he sat quietly and ate. When he had finished he got up to go, asking where Calvin was.

'He went to the Club,' was the reply, 'and afterwards he said he would be in the library at the British Museum.' Jude thought he wouldn't be seeing him much today then and replied that he, too, would be out all day, although he wasn't actually sure where he was going. Passing the sitting room he noticed a clock on the wall saying ten-thirty; no wonder his breakfast was cold.

Lily had a little more freedom than other servants in the area and as soon as Jude had left she picked up her broom and went outside to tidy her section of the street and catch up on any gossip. Jude's mannerisms and strangeness in general were becoming a hot topic.

Susie had slept in, but when she finally went downstairs the landlady felt sorry for her missing breakfast and told her to sit down and she would bring her some cold meat and coffee. For once she didn't feel hungry, which wasn't surprising after eating two meals the previous night, but she drank the coffee whilst she watched the landlady preparing breakfast for the other guests. The pleasant smell of hot toast and butter filled the air and for a moment she felt like she was staying in a Bed and Breakfast beside the sea. She liked it here, the pace was unhurried and no one asked any questions. After a while she folded the meat inside a loose piece of cloth that had been left on the table under some sugar tongs and stuffed it into her pocket. As she left the dining area she enquired whether the room would be available for a second night and was told that it was.

Feeling a little more secure she walked out of Oxford Street and back into Regent Street. The fresh piles of manure that were dotted around seemed particularly strong this morning. Roads and kerbs were being dampened down to keep the dust low. It was a partially sunny day and Susie had only just left the lodgings and started down the road when the little dog appeared again. Despite herself, she was really glad to see him, he was the one constant in this uncertain town and he managed to ease her sense of increasing desolation. She stopped at once and stroked his head between the ears, then gave him some of the meat she had saved for herself for later, and they walked along together. She stopped at a stand where a man was pouring out hot light brown liquid and to get a better view she stepped further into the gathering crowd. The sign nearby said '*Fresh and Refreshing Tonic*' and she could see the liquid was juice from tree bark. The seller was an elderly gentleman with a light grey beard and looked like he had confidence in his product. She had read recently that tree sap was being advocated as a new type of health food; a super drink – a complete pick-me-up packed with goodness. I'll try it, she thought, watching other people happily cradling their warm cups. It was 2d and tasted good and sweet.

Realising that she was coming up to the area that the animal trainer had been performing in, she diverted a little down a side street. The road was quieter and the houses more grand, all decorated with leaf patterned iron edging to the front. She approached the corner of a busy street and sat on the kerb, her head resting in her hands. She sat like this in a day dream, watching the crowds going about their business for almost an hour. Then, feeling more alert she stood up and stretched, her eyes focusing on a man in front of her who was sitting on a tall chair having his shoes polished thoroughly. He was idly reading the *Morning Chronicle* and as she walked by she stopped to read the writing on the front page. The headline across the top was a story about a recent robbery by a group of women which had led to murder. Further down was an interesting item which said that in order to help out the multitude of immigrants into London the South-Eastern railway were running a special daily two-way cross channel service. And then she saw it – blazoned in larger writing was an article in the bottom right hand corner with the headline 'S*trangers in our midst, or masters of forgery?*'

The article went on to say that police were exploring the strange incidences of unusual items being acquisitioned in London recently. The paper had printed all articles in parallel columns in English, French and German for all to see. She read on: '*Unexplained goods arriving in London, scientists brought in for an urgent meeting to evaluate*'. The first thing she saw was a description of the zip from her skirt and a feeling of nausea came over her. How stupid could she be? Zips weren't in use yet, she could see people were only wearing buttons. And worse, further down there were descriptions of Jude's watch and three of her charms. She didn't know Jude had lost his watch and hoped he was alright. Trying to clear her thoughts she reasoned that at least there were no pictures, and not everybody read the papers; but then she read the final part of the article, '*see separate poster for full description of these unusual items*' and a plea to the pawnbrokers:

'*We apply to honourable pawnbrokers that if you hold any other such items, to bring forth to the police.*' Susie scrambled through a group of people and went over to a boy who was holding a pile of newspapers. Her voice was urgent, 'there should be a separate poster, have you got any?'

The obliging boy tipped his pile of papers over and pulled a small poster out from underneath, 'here you are, they come with the paper, I just don't have many left.'

'I don't need the paper, thank you,' she replied almost snatching the poster from him and throwing a coin into his hands. 'Careful, ma'am I don't want 'em ripped.'

She apologised and went back to the corner of the quiet street and sat on a step nearby, scanning the poster in disbelief, smoothing out the creases so that she didn't miss a word.

This was much worse – there in front of her were illustrations of the zip, the watch and three of the charms. She cringed now when she saw them; to think that they thought these items would go unnoticed. The old fashioned telephone charm simply had one question mark above it and her boot charm, which was silver and purple, had a sentence underneath that read '*the boot has a theatrical colour; a tone of blue*'. Lastly the padlock charm, which she hadn't thought would cause any concern, had a picture of a key with question mark next to it in brackets; she knew now that it must have been an improved version, ahead of its time.

She thought back to the first pawnbroker they had visited. Now that she thought about it he had looked at the charm and then given her an odd look. The boot wasn't that unusual, a simple design with a very low heel, so it must have been the colour. She had seen most colours out on the street, vibrant yellows, reds, terracotta, green; but she hadn't seen purple. It could easily have been that pawnbroker who had alerted the authorities and others followed suit. She thought about the other charms, the telephone was another awful mistake, but how was she to know about the padlock? No wonder word was out – she hardly dared to read the rest.

At the bottom of the page there was an appeal for the public to read this carefully and be on the lookout for a gentleman and young lady of Jude and Susanna's description who behaved '*in an unconventional manner*'. It went on to suggest that the public look out for different vocabulary, or indeed references to anything as yet unknown, in order to verify descriptions of the offenders so that they may be brought for questioning. Susie folded the paper in half and half again and tucked it into her pocket. It all seemed a bit unfair, they were hardly murderers – or perhaps the authorities were afraid of what they could not understand; it must have been Jude's digital watch that pushed them to this – they were probably concerned about national security – and she couldn't really blame them.

She tried to be rational; there could be hundreds of people that fitted their descriptions should anyone come forward with a recollection. Yet in a moment of panic she made the decision to get rid of her final charm, the silver cat. She didn't want to be caught with it on her. She looked down at the little dog who had been steadfastly watching her. She gave him a hug and gently flattened his ears against his head, holding them in her hands. He looked up at her with his big soulful eyes and she whispered to him 'you're my pal now, you can wear it.' Taking a ribbon from her blouse pocket she threaded it through the link of the charm and tied it in a double bow under his collar, the charm showing only slightly; it was impossible to hide it completely. Her shoulders lowered with relief, at least she couldn't be incriminated and even though it was the most precious thing she owned, she still had the job for one more night.

Suddenly she felt sharp pains in her chest which cut through like a knife and within seconds had branched out sideward and upwards towards her throat. Taken aback by the ferocity of the gripping pain, she held on to the patchy, green railings for a few moments and then descended the five steps in front of a terraced house, lowering herself on to the corner step that partitioned the stairs. The pain eased a little when she sat, so she stayed there for a while, unable to inhale too deeply as this made it worse. A couple walked past and when the man saw her he tossed a coin over towards her. She didn't thank him; ashamed at what it must look like. It took so long for the pain to lessen that when she scrambled to the top of the stairs hoping to see if the little dog was still on the street, she was distraught to find he had gone. She thought he probably hadn't seen her go down the steps. It didn't matter that he had gone off with her charm, she was still glad to be rid of it, it was the fact that he had gone at all that made her bereft and before she could stop them, tears flooded her face. Still feeling a little tight in her chest, she went back down to the step, closed her eyes and rested.

CHAPTER THIRTEEN

Jude had left Calvin's chambers and began walking aimlessly. He still couldn't get over the low buildings – London without skyscrapers was a different place altogether; there was such a feeling of space, despite the chaos in the streets. It was an astronomer's dream; big skies and hardly any light pollution. But then he thought about the smog. It seemed to hang like a cloak over the Thames. During the dinner at the Club he had overheard that not only people but sometimes whole carriages fell in, they simply couldn't see the river's edge. He came towards Bond Street and decided to walk down it, which cheered him up considerably as this was indeed a fashionable looking area. The shops were well presented and classier and the street seemed less busy. He sauntered through it, taking in the furniture shops and perfumeries. One shop seemed larger than most, displaying furniture in the windows that pre-dated the Victorians. He looked at the name written above the shop front, *Phillips, specialising in fine arts and antiques*. He guessed it was an auction house judging by the arms and armour on display in adjacent windows, which also displayed a mishmash of porcelain and jewellery.

But all he could think about was Susie. His plan was to go back towards the Strand via Charing Cross. He had an instinct that she would have gone there as that was where they had both felt the most comfortable. He would pace up and down all day, if that's what it took. He became drawn to the hum of Piccadilly and when passing through was enticed towards the curve of The Quadrant at one end of Regent Street. He could already see the splendour of the Georgian apartments and decided to take a proper look while he was at this end of town.

This part of the street snaked round, The Quadrant being on the opposite side of the road. He stood and looked at the grand pillars supporting the curved building. The apartments were set back in a layer above with balconies to the front. Underneath was a covered walk way, no doubt ingenious for its day as many other shops made do with canopies hanging outside to cover their goods and to protect their customers. Jude noticed that Regent Street became busier on the approach to Oxford Street and the familiar street sellers were immediately upon him. He stopped at a stall selling stationery – it wasn't that he needed anything, but he noticed the seller was again elderly and obviously poor but had tried to dress well in a plaid waistcoat and top hat. Jude wanted to buy something, anything just to help him out. He assumed the seller didn't make much of a profit; he only had a few unbound books pegged across a piece of rope and some sheets of paper; Jude thought this must be because the tax on paper probably hadn't been lifted yet. He smiled at the seller and hastily bought a copy of last year's *Household Words*, giving him double the money he had asked for. The man was grateful, he smiled and nodded, reminding Jude of his own father and making him feel suddenly fearful at the thought of never seeing him again.

He felt something brush his trouser leg and looked down to see a small dog sniffing around his boots. He thought nothing of it and continued pointlessly wading through the stalls. The dog, however, was persistent and began to run in front of Jude, as though he was trying to trip him up. Irritated, Jude tried to evade the dog by snaking in and out of the stalls. But now the dog began barking, so in order to avoid drawing attention to himself Jude went back and stroked the top of his head lightly, 'what's your problem?' he said quietly. The dog shook his fur as if to give himself a clean and then Jude saw it

– the little silver cat charm tucked behind a ribbon around his collar.

'Wait a minute,' he said loudly, grabbing the dog with both hands so that he didn't get away. He kept still, his dark, mischievous eyes staring back at Jude.

'Come on,' he said urgently, 'show me where she is.' They walked quickly together through the crowds until the dog, with his tail wagging, turned a corner and ran towards some iron railings. His head was bent over some steps, looking downwards. By now Susie was propped up in a sitting position, with her eyes shut, but opened them as soon as she heard the dog panting. She saw someone approach and stand behind him and then she looked up to see Jude standing there. She could hardly believe it.

'Susie!' Jude shouted almost hysterically.

'Jude, thank goodness!' she replied. She got up as quickly as she could but was obviously wincing with pain. They held each other tight, swaying back and forth.

'Susie, I can't believe it – but what's the matter, are you hurt?' he asked holding her at arm's length so that he could take a good look at her. He looked down at the dog.

'And who's your friend?'

'I haven't given him a name, but he keeps following me.'

'Yeah, well he was obviously on my trail, I tried to lose him but he was very determined. Why did you tie the charm around his collar?'

Susie was about to explain but it was clear she was in discomfort.

'Was it something you ate?' asked Jude.

'No, I think it's the tree bark I had.'

'You drank tree bark?' asked Jude incredulously.

'I know, don't ask – it just looked warm and soothing and it must have been popular as there was a big crowd standing around drinking it,' she replied, attempting to smile.

'I'll find a pharmacy, not a quack doctor, we don't want to make things worse – what do you think it is, indigestion?'

'Yeah, could well be that, but I've never had it this bad before.'

'Okay, stay there,' he said twitching his feet, and then as an afterthought, 'here, you can read this, it'll take your mind off it.' He handed her the copy of *Household Words*.

'I won't be long, I'll ask someone.'

'Don't get lost, and Jude–' but he had already vanished. The dog came down to the step and sat with Susie. She put her arm round him and praised him and he settled into a ball and went to sleep.

Jude didn't waste any time, he asked someone for the nearest seller of potions straight away and followed the directions without stopping. He found a small shop with *Medicine Vendor* written above, and inside were countless bottles of ointments placed upon the shelves. He went straight to the counter.

'May I have something for heartburn, please?'

'Are you sure it's heartburn?' replied the woman serving.

'Well, indigestion then.'

'Is it for you?'

'No, it's for my sister.' It was the first thing he could think of to inform her of the gender.

'Did she eat or drink something unusual?'

'I don't know if it's unusual here, but she had tree sap.'

'Was it cold?'

'No, I think she said it was hot.'

'Then it must have been saloop,' said the woman and frowned, 'she probably needs to take some of this.' She went over to one of the shelves and brought over a bottle for Jude to see. She then opened it and wafted it towards his nose for him to sniff. It reminded him of a milky remedy his grandmother used to give him when he had an upset stomach.

He checked the label, *Pure Fluid Magnesia*, and thought it sounded alright and just nodded his approval.

'I'll prepare you some.' The woman went into a back room and took what seemed like ages.

She kept an eye on Jude and could see he was agitated; he seemed a little over anxious about a simple case of indigestion.

Bringing it over to the counter she said, 'don't worry it's probably only dyspepsia, everyone gets it.' She asked whether he wanted the small bottle for 1 shilling or larger for 2s and 6d. He chose the smaller one, paid and left. Afterwards she made a mental note of his description; she had seen the paper that morning and he was definitely unlike the usual people that came in here; although he could have been foreign but with exceptional English. She thought nothing more of it.

It didn't take him long to get back to Susie, he practically ran all the way for fear of losing her again and was relieved to see she hadn't moved from the spot.

'Here, take this,' he said handing her the little bottle.

'Thanks,' she sipped almost a third of it.

Jude looked down at the page Susie had been reading and saw *In Memorium* by one of her favourite poets, Lord Alfred Tennyson, and sat down beside her. She turned to him, full of enthusiasm, 'did you know he wrote this for his friend, Arthur Hallam, who died suddenly in his early twenties, it was a deep friendship, and some say he never got over it, it took him years to write the poem, not ever expecting to publish it.'

'Really?' replied Jude.

'Yes and Tennyson was a tall, heavy built man, who played with his children a lot, so did Prince Albert, but it was unusual at the time. He lived in Mablethorpe for a while; he absolutely loved the wild sweeping coastline, but he moved to the Isle of Wight.'

'Well I suppose it makes sense, wasn't he the Poet Laureate

last year?' asked Jude, happily joining in, he had missed these discussions.

Susie nodded and then went quiet. Jude watched her expression change.

'What's up?' he asked. She couldn't put it off any longer, and reached inside her pocket and brought out the poster – she didn't want to spoil their joyful moment of reunion, but he had to know.

'You need to see this,' she said unfolding it, 'it's a flyer that came with today's paper.' Jude stared at the drawings, finding it hard to register what he was seeing.

'They've got hold of my watch, how on earth did they get it?' he said and impulsively took off his boot and sock, shaking it out to check that his £1 coin wasn't missing as well.

'Your charms,' he continued 'I didn't think they would cause such a fuss, I mean, a padlock? I thought they would be using them.'

'I know,' agreed Susie, 'but we should have known better about the telephone, and what about purple? I haven't seen any purple.'

They were silent for a moment. Jude couldn't believe they had overlooked the telephone – they had been concentrating so hard on surviving that they hadn't been thinking clearly. They looked at the little dog that was still sleeping, his body moving up and down in rhythm with his relaxed breathing.

'Susie, I'm going to take the silver cat off his collar, we may need it.'

'Yes, I suppose – I just panicked, I didn't want to be incriminated.' The dog didn't seem to notice, he was sleeping so deeply.

'I understand,' he said, giving her another hug, 'it's just great to see you – what have you been doing anyway?'

'I've got a job,' she replied with a grin, 'in a restaurant.'

'What? You've got a job, what did you do, fake some references?'

'Well I know that's what they tend to do here, but no I didn't have to, I was mistaken for someone else I think – it was good fun and I got to eat a very noble dinner.'

'What's it called?'

'Verrey's.'

'I think I might have passed it today, it looked like a very grand place.'

'Well, I'm supposed to go back there at five o'clock and work this evening.'

'Do you want to?' asked Jude.

'In a funny way, yes, I really enjoyed it and it kept me busy while I was worrying about you.'

'Well, if you're up to it, why don't you go? I'll come with you and wait right outside until you've finished and then we can go and celebrate finding each other again. I've sampled the night life, it's awesome!'

'Yes, I've seen some of it; I went out with some of the kitchen staff to a supper room where they served oysters and champagne, although I had grog.'

'Grog?'

'Yes, I'll save that for another time, tell me what you've been doing – how did you lose your watch?'

Jude wasn't sure where to begin; but told her about his near strangulation whilst being robbed when they were parted, and the next day finding a football match and meeting his new friend, Calvin.

'I can't believe you were invited to stay in someone's posh chambers!' said Susie impressed.

'It was rather smart, and there is a maid, Lily.' He thought for a moment. 'Come to think of it, she was asking me a lot of questions, I think she may already suspect me. She said she had brought some water up to my room but I was asleep, she could have been snooping around.'

'I don't think it's anything to be concerned about, more

worrying are the descriptions of us, what if all our encounters with the public have been analysed and they are now on our trail?' replied Susie. Jude was shaking his head, 'I don't believe it for a minute, there are thousands of people passing through every street and a lot of them must look like us.'

They agreed to be cautious but not let it spoil their adventure and stayed put and caught up until Susie's pain had more or less gone. It wasn't long before Jude became really hungry again. He could hear the cry of 'baked potatoes, all 'ot' from a vendor and suggested they get one. But Susie declined, deciding to give her stomach a rest and sat on some sleepers watching Jude buy his. It came with just butter, but was now a firm favourite with him. She was happy again now and had begun to appreciate this raw, chaotic street life despite an underlying sense of resignation of its people. Here she was mingling with many other Londoners who appeared to eat most of their meals on the street. It was mid-afternoon again and already some street entertainers were swinging into action. This time they could hear bagpipes in the distance and in nearby eateries clatters of pots and pans could be heard where, if you glanced in the open doorways, men with their shirt sleeves rolled up were beginning preparation for the evening visitors who preferred to dine indoors.

'Let's go and find Calvin, I want to tell him I've found you,' said Jude excitedly. Susie felt more apprehensive, but agreed, and they began walking, taking care to avoid the perilous Seven Dials district, eventually nearing the edge of Lincoln's Inn Fields. The central area was left untouched and clear, it was more or less the same as they knew it, but the British Museum building itself made them both stop in their tracks. It was the same magnificent building, but stood out so much more because the surrounding buildings were far more insignificant. The lack of high rise buildings in general was what they were both growing to love about this London along with the fact that they weren't ever too far from any fields. They went into the entrance hall and one of the first things they noticed were three life size giraffes in the corner of the first row of stairs. Jude turned to Susie, 'we haven't really got time to look around, we'll have to go straight to the library.' They were following directions but just as they were getting nearer, Calvin happened to see them.

'Jude,' he called quietly, 'what are you doing here?' Jude turned around excitedly.

'We were coming to find you, though it would have been a disaster, you wouldn't have been in there, obviously!'

'It's closed in the first week of September, I forgot, I've just been exploring the rooms whilst I'm here.' He looked over at Susie, and smiled curiously.

'Who's this?' he said.

'That's what I came to tell you – this is Susanna, my cousin, I found her.' His elation was infectious.

'Oh my goodness, Susanna, I've heard all about you,' said Calvin bringing her hand to his mouth and kissing it. Susie liked him immediately, his brown eyes shone sincerely and she knew how helpful he'd been towards Jude.

'Hello, likewise, any friend of Jude's is a friend of mine,' she said rather too cheerily, she knew it sounded modern, but she was thrilled – this was the first time they had been on genuine friendly terms with another Victorian since they had arrived.

'You must come to my parents' house for dinner this evening,' said Calvin, continuing his generous hospitality.

'Well–' said Jude, not sure at all, looking to Susie for an answer.

'Yes, thank you. That is very kind,' she replied.

'Settled then. They live in Gower Street, the house three doors from the end with the green door; you can't miss it – seven o'clock,' he said walking away. After a few paces he looked back over his shoulder before turning the corner and was surprised to see them looking at each other so intimately, with Jude squeezing Susanna's hand – cousins indeed, he thought and then wondered why they would go to such lengths to be untruthful.

Standing outside the British Museum they paused for a moment. Susie took a good look around, admiring the huge trees but couldn't help but notice how choked with smoke some of the leaves seemed to be and there was an oppressive heaviness in the atmosphere that she hadn't noticed before. It seemed a crime that magnificent new buildings like these were being gradually charred by coal. Something else had caught Jude's attention. He had noticed men coming and going through a couple of outdoor privies. He pointed them out to Susie.

'You're kidding!' was all she could say.

'No, I'm going to take a look.' He wasn't gone long.

'Don't bother, it's disgusting. They are a type of toilet, but they don't flush, so you can imagine.' Susie could – she had been to enough outdoor concerts to know how awful it got when the toilets eventually stopped working. It just wasn't worth it.

Jude was thinking about the restaurant and wondered how they were going to manage to fit it all in in time.

'You don't owe them anything, just make the sauces and leave,' he said.

'I know I don't have to go at all, but I like it there and I had good fun with them last night. Anyway I will explain that I only have two hours and can only make the basic sauces and will then have to leave.'

'Okay, then let's get a cab and go straight there.'

CHAPTER FOURTEEN

They arrived about three-thirty. Jude watched Susie go in and be greeted by a chef; she was early and he could see her explaining something and the chef nodding. As she disappeared further into the kitchen she turned and gave a 'thumbs up' to him. Feeling more relaxed; he perched on a large, empty overturned urn and sat with his back against a wall. There was a chill in the air, he had noticed that in general since being here the sun shone quite brightly in the mornings but then faded away as the day wore on, leaving the smoky air clinging on like damp talons. Still, he had his copy of *Household Words* and turned to read one of the instalments of *David Copperfield* to keep himself occupied. The time passed quickly and when he was tired of reading he had sat and watched the comings and goings on the main street but then the door to the kitchen opened and one of the chefs beckoned him inside.

'Come, come, ça va? Susanna has just told me she has a friend out here – come and enjoy our delicious coffee.' It was just what Jude needed; he jumped off the urn quickly. Susie was inside talking to the others and he went over and joined them. Again there were no introductions, such was the transient nature of the employment around here and anyway there was no need. Susie had told him before how the French chefs in particular were always generous to strangers and to the poor, making sure that any leftover food at the end of service each day was given out to them directly or via the soup kitchens and he could see for himself the charitable nature of all the staff. Susie said she had finished her shift and Jude emptied his cup; the coffee was indeed superior to any he had tasted here yet. They said their farewells as time was getting on and they wanted their stroll to the dinner at Gower Street to be a leisurely one. Outside the streets were beginning to fill with parading entertainers and many groups of musicians whose music made the streets come alive, particularly as they neared taverns where the overspill of people into the streets filled the air with alcoholic fumes. Across the road someone shouted 'oi shut up' and threw something at a singer who was slightly out of tune.

'Was that a dead animal?' asked Susie tearfully.

'Yes, I think it was – come on, let's move away from here.'

Jude took Susie to see The Quadrant to take their minds off it and she, too, was stunned at the grand architectural style, with its row of imposing pillars positioned round in an elegant weave.

'It's a shame buildings like this got knocked down,' she said.

'I know, I don't know the reason, maybe the design became outdated or something, but it's been rebuilt in a similar style.' Before long they had sauntered into Knightsbridge and were surprised at how slummy it was. The droves of women and soldiers hanging around the entrance to the military encampment were becoming a familiar sight. Susie shuddered as she saw the tangled unkempt hair of the women and their dirty hands and faces. As they went past they could overhear some of them.

'My father says it's the first time there's been a record of occupations.'

'What did you put down?' They were all giggling at the answers and Susie strained to hear that some had put needleworker and others shawlfringemaker. One boasted that she had even put governess which was received with applause and rapturous shrieking. Once they were clear of them Jude whispered to Susie.

'Do you remember the census a decade or so ago – my Dad used to refer to it?'

'No, what about it?'

'Apparently loads of people put Jedi Knight under the section for religion.'

'It does ring a bell,' she replied and couldn't help but smile – some things never seem to change – you could go back hundreds of years and people will be people. Jude stopped in his tracks suddenly and looked up, 'Look at that!' he said.

'What, anybody would think you'd seen a dinosaur or something,' said Susie bending over trying to knock mud from her boot.

'No, not at this Exhibition, but they are at the next.' Realising what he meant she looked up immediately and saw a massive glass and iron structure that housed the Great Exhibition. They could see large trees inside it, through the glass. They were stunned and couldn't understand why they hadn't noticed it before; the building was immense and extraordinary.

'We must come back here tomorrow,' said Jude.

'Yes, we must, just don't get dragged off when I'm looking the other way again! Stick to me like glue.' She was serious. He put his arm around her and they changed direction towards the Strand where they were soon amongst the familiar sights and sounds of the days they spent together before they were parted. The streets became even busier with the tantalising smell of chops and steaks being broiled or seared on gridirons. Excitement from audiences was palpable as acrobats and jugglers began entertaining the crowds. One conjurer was wearing silky bright red shorts and had actually discarded his hat, but, as was becoming the norm, something inspirational was followed by something equally dreadful.

'Oh no, look at this,' said Susie disbelieving; it was a dancing bear. 'I can't look, it's awful.' Jude watched anyway but felt really uncomfortable and blurted something out about laws against cruelty to animals.

'Shush, keep your voice down,' said Susie who was now much more afraid of being noticed. They moved quickly on and began again to get caught up in the spirit of the street entrepreneurs. To their right, walking amongst the crowds, were two people carrying the front part of a roll of canvas. Drawn on it was scenery that resembled a trip down the Nile. Jude suggested they walk at the same pace to see the picture unravel in front of them. There were sand dunes and sand storms and then a picture of a small city appeared. It went on for about a mile, when somebody from the crowd, possibly a native of the area being shown, ran up to the person unwinding the picture. He looked a little irritated at some of the details and began pointing them out. The canvas holders paused and the person who had sketched it seemed to listen with patience and care, taking the criticism in good faith and then changing the drawing accordingly. The canvas continued on with people walking alongside watching it slowly unravelling.

'I suppose this is one way of bringing tourism to the public when most people couldn't afford to go abroad,' said Jude, he couldn't really think why else they would do it.

'I suppose…' Susie was distracted; she couldn't quite get over the painstaking detail of the panorama. They watched it disappear and then deviated off towards the direction of the dinner party.

'Are you wearing cologne?' asked Susie.

'Yes, I bought some in a small perfumery earlier.'

'Can I have some please; I could use something to help me freshen up for this dinner.'

'Course,' said Jude passing the little bottle over. Susie splashed it all over herself liberally and handed it back.

When they arrived at Gower Street she halted, putting her

hand across Jude's chest to slow him down as well. Three men were coming out of one of the houses, laughing and joking. They were all quite young looking; one of them had long, wavy hair and a delicate looking face, and the other two were similar looking but with hair settling around their ears and with wide side partings. Their suits were in unusual colours.

'They fit the descriptions–' Susie began excitedly, but stopped mid-sentence when she realised after scrutinising them, that the man with the long hair was the same man she had met at the gallery in the Pantheon Bazaar. She wasn't certain at all, but now seeing him as part of a group–. Embarrassed, she made sure they kept their distance behind them and said nothing to Jude.

'Of who?' said Jude, his curiosity was aroused.

'Do you remember the Pre-Raphaelite Brotherhood? Dante Gabriel Rossetti, William Holman Hunt and I can't remember the third one, but it looks just like them.'

'Really?' Jude would never have pieced this together, but had heard of them, 'weren't they famous because their paintings were more modern, like life portraits of women with big eyes?'

'Well, yes, but it wasn't all about the women and it wasn't all modern, they painted subjects from literature too, I suppose their paintings stood out because they were trying to tell part of a story,' said Susie who had begun whispering.

'Not sure what you mean,' said Jude frowning, and wondering why Susie was being so guarded. She was about to explain, but two of the men parted company with the third man, who, to Susie's relief was not the man with long hair.

He continued walking in the direction that Jude and Susie were going in, suddenly noticing them. It became obvious that they were all heading for the house where the dinner was being held, only a few steps away. After knocking they waited awkwardly together on the same step, but the door was soon opened by a servant, and Calvin was standing behind, quick to welcome them. Jude had mentioned to Susie how Calvin had sensed his unease and witnessed his bouts of idiocy when joining new social circles and she suddenly felt vulnerable herself. As she caught sight of herself in the mirror she felt shocked at how bedraggled she looked and quickly removed her cape and shawl and loosened her blouse, pulling it off around her shoulders for an appropriate evening look, she ran her fingers through her hair to tidy it.

They were escorted to the dining room, which was up the stairs and into the first room on the right, and seated with the other guests around the long, elegantly decorated table. Luckily as they were the last to arrive, they were seated at the end, where there was less chance of being the centre of attention. Jude was placed opposite Susie, with Calvin next to her and an elegantly dressed young lady next to Jude. Large silver candlesticks held tall candles which had already been lit and wine was being poured by a footman whose hair was tied back. He was wearing a brightly coloured jacket, with tapered trousers tucked into long white socks. Other servants were crowding in the doorway.

Calvin stood up.

'Some introductions, if I may.' He went round the table relaying the names of various people and describing their occupations. Susie heard the words 'scientist' and 'physician' but couldn't remember the rest. She watched Calvin, who was concluding.

'And these are my new friends, Jude and Susanna, who are cousins visiting from the country.' He turned to look at the lady next to Jude.

'And this is my sister, Lorena, and next to her our special guest, John Everett Millais.' Susie's eyes widened as she grinned at Jude trying to mouth the words 'Brotherhood'. Jude understood, although knew little about them and his mind drifted back to college and whether he was absent when the topic of nineteenth century art was being discussed.

The atmosphere in the room was relaxed. People were talking in small groups and the waiters were busy pacing up and down. Jude saw Susie looking perplexed at the array of cutlery in front of her and he said quietly, 'just watch me, I've done this before.' She nodded gratefully and looked around at the ornate room with its deep green velvet curtains enveloping the double windows that looked on to the street. Pale green wallpaper patterned with small flowers covered the walls. In one corner stood an elegant glass cabinet with silver ornaments inside and hanging on the walls were all sorts of portraits, some in gilt-edged frames. Directly ahead of her was a large mahogany sideboard being busily attended by servants. She noticed a large wooden knife case about a foot high and a foot deep with slots for holding cutlery. She had heard one of the servants mention 'flatware' but wasn't sure what that meant. The case was tapered to the front with veneer flowered edging; she hadn't seen anything like it before. Other items were slightly more recognisable, a large, yet delicate silver breadbasket with handle that looped right over and brass gravy jugs.

Before they arrived Jude and Susie had agreed that to minimise bringing attention to themselves they would try to sit quietly, speak only when spoken to and most importantly to think before they spoke. Luckily they had a clear view of each other and could correspond, but views of some of the guests were obstructed by a large central display of fruit and green foliage woven around a three tiered stand. The tablecloth was a pristine white colour and dotted around it were delicate decanters containing some kind of alcohol. Jude opened his serviette and a small roll fell on to the table. Bowls of pale cream coloured soup were being served by some of the waiters, while others stood in attendance behind. Susie began eating, not knowing what to expect but thought she could taste chicken and almonds and thought it was very good. As she was finishing she noticed Jude lift up his small glass and look directly over at her. She nodded and picked up the correct glass when the sherry came round.

'So,' began one guest to the physician, 'how are the refugees faring in Leicester Square?'

'Oh, very well I hear,' the physician replied. 'The French in particular have opened many cafes, allowing plenty of work for waiters and it seems the Frenchmen happily reside together, be they rich or poor.' There was a murmur of praise and relief amongst the diners. Susie couldn't help herself, knowing that if this crowd didn't know where her favourite chef was, she wasn't sure who would.

'And what of the renowned French chef Alexis Soyer?' she asked.

'Well, he's been striving to take guests after they have seen the Exhibition on an extravagant gastronomic journey,' replied Calvin's mother, 'but he may have been too ambitious, and is making a bit of a loss, I'm afraid.'

'Oh,' was all Susie could think to say, not understanding at all. Another guest continued, 'yes, he means well, and his attention to detail is out of this world, but whether his licence will be allowed to continue after the Exhibition closes is another matter.' Susie didn't pursue the subject, as by now she had gathered he was somewhere near the Exhibition and would find out soon enough. Meanwhile oysters had appeared on the table along with plates piled high with whitebait, trout, salmon, and two other dishes that she didn't recognise.

'Chablis, madam?' asked the waiter. Susie glanced at Jude who held the coloured glass up.

'Yes, thank you,' she replied lifting her own blue glass. Jude had begun talking to Lorena; he seemed comfortable, no doubt because she had the same relaxed manner as Calvin.

'Could you pass the John Dory please?' asked John Millais looking directly at Susie. She scanned the two unknown dishes; one was in a liquid, and the other – she was clearly unsure but Calvin quickly reached over her and picked up the yellow coloured fish, 'there you are, I'd try the carp stew afterwards, it's very good,' and gave a sideward nod at Susie. This must be what Jude had experienced; Calvin had a knack of coming to the rescue at the right moment.

Calvin turned to Susie, a little surprised at how she was cutting up her food, and began questioning her about her background. She replied carefully but knew by his response that it wasn't what he was expecting. She had obviously given a slightly different account of their past to Jude's. Calvin, however, glossed over it and there was a natural pause in conversation around the room as plates were cleared for the next entrée. When it arrived they witnessed a flamboyant display of all kinds of meats, accompanied by patties, rissoles, stewed celery and sea kale. Susie decided to take it slowly and have very small amounts; she knew that every conceivable type of meat must be here on the table at the same time. She didn't want her awful indigestion to return, but as she ate less, she found she was sipping more to remain occupied because of the need to stay calm. The accompanying drink this time was champagne, which she knew would be poured into the flute glasses. She began cutting the asparagus on her plate and Jude caught her attention by clearing his throat quite loudly. She watched him pick his knife and fork up to cut the tips off and then purposefully cast his knife aside, using only his fork to eat them. What a palaver this was turning out to be, thought Susie, but she painstakingly copied him. All diners now joined in the main conversation at the table. The scientist was speaking.

'I see there is a lecture on the state of the Thames Tunnel next Wednesday. I have been down there; not for the faint-hearted, too many steep stairs!'

'What exactly is down there?' asked another guest.

The scientist explained, 'well, not an awful lot, really – it is rather strange, there are the usual stalls and small shops, mostly run by elderly women, and then there are a few competitions, you know for the strongest man, that kind of thing. But there is a very gloomy atmosphere down there; it is as though they are trying to create fun in a hollow empty shell under the ground.' Another man joined in.

'And it is only for pedestrians – I mean there is plenty of room for carriages, but apparently the company could not afford to build the roads leading to the tunnel, so it is a bit empty and almost ghostly.'

'Is there a charge?' asked Calvin's father, adding 'not that I would go down there now even if it was free.' There was muffled laughter.

'Oh yes, 2d I think and a lot more for the carriages, but it is unpopular because people say that those who go down there cannot shake off that vulnerable feeling, you know, you can hear the tidal Thames crashing against the sides of the tunnel as you walk, and the thought of a possible breach brings people out in a cold sweat.'

'That's not surprising,' said Lorena, shuddering at the thought.

By now Jude and Susie were exchanging confused looks. Neither of them had heard of an underground tunnel, and couldn't believe it had already been achieved.

'So, in theory, you have taken the brave decision to walk through the tunnel, arrived at Wapping, and what then?' asked Calvin's father, looking around the table.

'Precisely, just mud and planks, not good for the dresses,' said his mother trying to lighten up the conversation. Susie quite liked her. The champagne kept on flowing and one of the guests asked for a decanter to be passed over. 'Sure,' said Susie who went to pick it up amid a momentary silence as the conversation halted. Lorena leaned in Susie's direction.

'We don't usually pick up the decanters.' She was smiling when she spoke but there were a few disapproving glances around the room as the conversation was now centred on the special guest, John Millais who was trying to defend Ruskin's appreciation of the work of the Pre-Raphaelites.

'He considers a lot of painting to be stale, you know, cows in ditches, white sails; he agrees with the notion that art needs to be more inspired by emotion and to be atmospheric.'

Millais went on to give a detailed description of the way he himself approached an oil painting and how he would invite people to pose for him. Then he began talking about *Hamlet* and Susie thought that at least she could join in, knowing the play quite well. He was explaining how he was thinking of portraying Ophelia as a fusion of nature. But Susie wasn't concentrating, as soon as she heard the name Ophelia her mind went straight to how Queen Gertrude's description of her decline and fall into the river was depicted in the painting. Millais was portraying the exact same subject to the rest of the diners when Susie chipped in.

'Why did you paint her with her eyes looking upwards, it makes it kind of weird, it's bad enough that she's floating in the water fully clothed?' Jude didn't immediately see what was wrong with the question until he heard the gasps around the table. Millais simply put his glass down and stared at her in a disconsolate way.

'Try to see the melancholia,' but then he stalled for a second, 'just a moment – I have not yet completed it; in fact I have barely begun. I am sketching the background first and then I intend to come to London to begin the portrait and so my question to you is how could you possibly know how I was going to interpret this scene?'

Oh no, thought Susie, looking apologetically over at Jude who frowned at her slightly.

'Oh, I was calling your bluff,' she said quickly back-pedalling, 'it was just guesswork, most people are aware that Ophelia drowned by stumbling into the water whilst she was singing; why wouldn't you paint the reality of that?' She tailed off before she gave anything else away. She could see his vexed expression as he stared at his napkin. There was an awkward silence, but then the desserts arrived and the conversation went back to its previous tone. Susie thought it better not to look at anyone and purposefully became engrossed in the delights that were travelling across the room as if in a convoy; each one as impressive as the last. Among them were two-toned jellies, Spanish pudding, fruit tarts and custard puddings. Ices followed and she was told that the flavours were of pine, orange and ginger. The waiters came around again with more drinks and she watched as Jude was asked 'claret, port or Madeira, sir?' Jude replied 'Madeira, please,' raising the correct glass as he looked over at Susie. When asked the same she was equipped with the right glass and just repeated what Jude had said, although she now felt a little wobbly and sensed that she had had more than enough to drink. As if on cue, the topic of conversation had now changed to the social problem of excessive drinking and one guest sat with his arms folded as if he was about to address a meeting.

'Well, it is a big problem indeed, and what about the ladies out in the evening – foreign travellers have taken to writing of their accounts in England; I know there is a similar problem in Holland and Germany, but it is England that interests the Europeans the most; that all ages and genders take to the drink. It may be highly amusing to tourists, but it is a huge problem for the government and their Laissez-faire attitude will get them nowhere.'

Jude was shuffling restlessly in his seat and Susie cringed as she knew that frustrated look, and sure enough he began in earnest.

'Yeah, and it doesn't change, it just gets worse, not the prostitution, although that goes on for decades, but the drinking, jeez–' Susie tried waving at him but he didn't see her. She bent her head as he continued, 'it doesn't matter how hard we try, no one can solve the problem – no one – let's face it, it must simply be that we don't know how to drink, no wonder the tourists are laughing.' He paused when he had felt a sudden blow to his shin, he looked over at Susie who had slid down her chair in order to prod his leg with her boot to try and get him to stop. He got the message and changed the subject quickly, 'have you all visited the Exhibition? The end of season must soon be upon us?'

'Oh yes,' came the replies and the table was alight with enthusiastic discussion about the vast collection of oddities and futuristic exhibits for all to see. The electric telegraph was mentioned and there was general agreement about the obscure choice of allowing a young boy to run the demonstration hourly during the day.

'It's a good invention,' interrupted Jude, 'but soon all of Europe gets disrupted when a solar flare causes a storm surge. We're still not sure what causes them; solar storms certainly are an enigma.' Jude was on a roll; Susie just put her head in her hands in despair and Lorena was smiling at him in an amused way, but she was the only one.

'I beg your pardon?' asked Calvin's father.

Calvin decided it was time to interrupt.

'He always does this, goes off on a bit of a tangent, making things up to get the attention of the crowd, it is often down to too many sherry cobblers, he'll go quiet in a minute, won't you old boy?' he said looking sternly over at Jude. There was an awkward silence and then a few of the women tried to laugh it off, mainly to again revive the atmosphere at the dinner table. The desserts were eaten to more muffled voices and tranquil conversation in general and then the waiters brought out finger bowls filled with rosewater. Susie instinctively felt like plunging both hands in and splashing them around, giving them a well-earned wash. Instead she copied Lorena who dipped the side of her napkin in one of them and dabbed her mouth.

A variety of cheeses were now being placed on the table. Susie couldn't resist cheese and automatically leaned over Calvin, cut a chunk and put it on to her plate, but Calvin caught her arm and moved it away and goaded her into joining the ladies as they all got up from the table to withdraw to another room. Susie reluctantly got up as well, looking over at Jude who was shaking his head and mouthing 'no cheese for ladies'. She nodded in confirmation and he watched her disappear and wished it was time to go, but he managed to sit it out for another half an hour without any gaffs and then made his excuses to Calvin and his father.

In the other room the women were creating a mini play to act out to the gentlemen when they joined them by the fire, but Susie declined to join in, insisting she just wanted to watch and settled in one of the more comfortable looking chairs. It was fun to watch them audition each other for parts and then begin to improvise, but she was glad when Jude came and found her and she could see he was equally relieved that the evening was almost over. She smiled as gracefully as she could at the women, after the concoction she had eaten and drunk, and went over to particularly thank Lorena and her mother, excusing herself for missing the rest of the evening's entertainment. The air was chilly as they stepped outside but they were escorted to a waiting Hackney coach and the driver told them he was to take them home and that the fare was taken care of.

'Well, that was disastrous,' said Jude once they were sitting inside out of earshot.

'You're telling me,' replied Susie sternly. They exchanged awkward glances.

'Where are we going?' he asked.

'Oxford Street, I've got lodgings there for a second night.'

'Thank goodness for that.' They slunk into the warmth of the carriage, gradually relaxing to the rhythm of the horses' hooves. There was a light fog enveloping the rooftops and chimneys again. They watched the dimly gaslit streets trying to compete with it and could see the flickering brighter lights in the distance where the major nightspot areas were. They passed a tavern where people, mostly women, had started spilling into the street in a show of gaiety, dancing and laughing in a circle, oblivious to the men standing around, watching with interest as though this were all part of the London scene that shouldn't be missed, and as they drove into the livelier streets, pockets of drunkenness became apparent almost everywhere.

In Gower Street the male guests were still sat at the dining table and when they heard that Jude and Susanna had left Calvin's father turned to Calvin and began asking questions about them. How did he meet them? Was there anything unusual about their clothes? What about their accents and their intuitive behaviour that was so different from their own? Calvin was reluctant to speak. He had noticed that they were very different, but refused to believe it. He remembered seeing Jude's shirt collar the other day, never seen anything quite like it. His father was becoming impatient.

'Jude stayed at your chambers, you must have something to add?' he said, gruffly.

'Well,' Calvin replied, 'Lily did tell me that the night Jude went to bed exhausted she took him up a hot brandy cup, but he was already asleep. She looked over at his carelessly discarded pile of clothes and her eyes fell towards his socks and boots. One of his socks had been turned inside out and there was a coin on the floor. She picked it up and was surprised at how unusual it was; it looked like it was made of gold but apart from that she had seen nothing like it before. She called me to the room and I too picked it up and inspected it. I didn't recognise the face on the engraving and the thickness of the coin was startling, it was as though it didn't belong here at all–'

'Well, have you got it?' asked one of the guests.

'No, no, I couldn't take it; in fact I put it back in his sock so that he didn't suspect anything in the morning.' Calvin's father was rubbing his chin, deep in thought.

'Do you think this is connected with the other unusual pieces of silver that the whole town seems to be looking for?' asked the scientist.

'One couldn't say,' replied another guest, 'there was no mention of a coin on the poster, but it does seem a strange coincidence.'

'What other silver pieces?' Calvin asked his father who by way of reply walked over to the bureau and retrieved a small poster which he gave to his son. Calvin looked carefully at the other items, but had not seen any of them and they were of no relevance as far as he could see. He looked at them again and thought how charming they were; the intricate shapes and extraordinary detail; none of this made any sense.

'I'll see what I can do,' he said nonchalantly, 'I will arrange to see them again and notify the police so that they may question them.' In truth he hadn't actually arranged to meet with them ever again and did not intend to do so. They were his friends and he wished them well. His father smiled appreciatively.

'Well then, another liquor gentlemen?'

༈

Susie and Jude arrived at the lodgings, thanked their driver and waited until he had left. Jude was about to follow Susie inside, but she was cautious.

'You never know what the rules are, so to be safe you'd better not show yourself. I'll go in first and then when it's all clear I'll come back down and let you in.' She looked left and right for somewhere for him to hide.

'Wait round the corner.' She knocked at the door and waited for the landlady to come. Few words were spoken as it was quite late and Susie went straight upstairs. She looked out of the window and could see the street was a lot quieter, she made some noise as though she were taking her boots off and then checked to see if the corridors were clear. She waited a moment or two more and then went straight back down, leaving the front door ajar. She gave a quiet whistle and to her surprise the little dog came running up to her from nowhere.

'Oh, no,' she said to him, but was secretly thrilled that he hadn't forgotten them. She gave him such a big hug she nearly flattened him, but he didn't seem to mind, he was just standing there panting in response. Then Jude strolled up behind wondering what the muffled commotion was.

'Oh, oh, where did he come from? This only means more trouble, next we'll be accused of stealing him, and we can't take many more risks.' He wasn't joking.

'Er, that's already happened, I'll tell you about it tomorrow. Come on in, quickly.' He followed her into the house and tiptoed upstairs. When the driver and carriage returned to Gower Street Calvin's parents made a note of the address that Jude and Susanna had asked to be taken to.

CHAPTER FIFTEEN

It was Saturday morning and as Calvin gathered a few things for his journey he was aware that Lily had been up and about bright and early giving more details of the curiosity surrounding Jude to other occupants in the street. He knew that the poster had been passed around but Lily did not know, she had said, that there was a girl involved. She was testing him, but he would not allow himself to tell her that he had met Jude's 'cousin', Susanna. He had looked out the window and seen the tall muffin-seller walk past doing his early morning rounds. He was carrying them in a box over one shoulder and calling loudly and repetitively that they were all delicious and hot. He always stopped to chat, and no doubt he would tell those in the next street about the enigmatic young man wandering freely about the neighbourhood.

Lily had tried to talk to Calvin about Jude's awkwardness, almost acting like a foreigner when he clearly wasn't, but Calvin refused to get caught in a conversation about it. He felt an affinity with Jude and had told him that he was welcome to stay any time and that the invitation extended to Susanna as well, but did not envisage he would see them again as they were generally very elusive. Perhaps they had seen the posters too and were now much more wary. He knew they fitted the descriptions perfectly and that they were definitely displaced. In fact he had no idea where they really came from and worried that they would not be safe night or day now, and he felt quite helpless. Anyway it wasn't going to spoil his plans. He was off to Brighton for the day trying out the new railways. He would pick up some reading material at the station and drop it off when he disembarked. It was an exciting new trend. He was looking forward to some much needed sea air that the physician had recommended to him the previous evening; that is if there was room for him amongst the carriages laden with families on one side and courtesans on the other.

Jude and Susie got up at dawn. Space in the room had been tight and whilst Susie had slept tucked comfortably in the bed, Jude had perched on the outside edge all night, trying not to fall off. But he didn't mind, it was a great relief to be back together. They crept out before the owners of the house became aware that Jude had stayed there at all.

An hour after they had left, two policemen were making enquires at the Oxford Street lodging house. It was still early, but the landlady was up and had gone to the room to check on Susanna. She went back to the door and informed them that she had already left without having breakfast. When asked if it was possible that she had been accompanied by a young man the landlady insisted they had got the wrong person. She thought Susanna was rather quiet, but other than that she genuinely didn't know what their enquiries were about.

The day was glimmering with the early morning sun and in the adjacent roads street sweepers and milkmaids could be seen; their donkeys pulling the carts slowly and laboriously. Quiet animal sounds echoed through the streets and cockerels could be heard in the distance. It was strange, Susie still couldn't adjust to the fact that they were in the city, defined by routines such as these, yet they could easily have been on a farm. A few people were queuing at a large water pump with urns in their hands. The little dog, which had been lying down outside the front door when they came out, had jumped up and joined them as soon as they moved. He was always a welcome sight and by now Susie was sure he had shunned his owner, the animal trainer, preferring Jude and Susie as his caretakers. They both patted and stroked him and he walked alongside them, his tail wagging contentedly. Susie studied him; he was a sturdy little dog, his golden, wavy fur was amazingly clean. She watched his cute lobular ears flop along to the rhythm of his steps. He always appeared optimistic and affectionate.

She turned to Jude, 'this really should be our final day. What do you want to do with it?'

'Shall we do the whole tourist thing, starting with Madame Tussauds; neither of us have been,' he replied enthusiastically.

'Why not, but we'll have to get to Baker Street.'

'Baker Street?'

'Yes, that's where it was before it was moved to Marylebone Road,' said Susie, 'apparently she had a travelling exhibition for years before she settled here and–' but Jude wasn't listening – he was tapping his hat to remove some debris before placing it back on his head.

By now the sound of shutters opening was echoing all around and breakfast stalls were being set up on the roads and pavements and all areas were quickly filling up with people. The irresistible smell of bacon drifted through the air and Jude and Susie stopped, purchased some and placed it in two rolls, perching on old boxes as they ate them. They asked for bread soaked in milk for the dog.

'Right, where's Baker Street?' asked Jude.

'I know where it should be, it's just recognising the way from here,' said Susie.

'Well, let's walk towards Regent Park, but there's not time to go to the zoo–'

'No, I know,' said Susie interrupting him, 'I'd love to see how similar it is, though, and I'd like to see the new giraffe that had to walk all the way from Blackwall.'

'Well, most of the animals seem to be wandering through the streets freely anyway, not sure why they bothered with the zoo,' said Jude 'and they're better behaved than some of the people!' Susie smiled. They purposefully walked along the edge of the road where the omnibuses passed and it wasn't long before Susie was almost scooped up by the conductor with Jude following closely behind, but then he remembered the dog and leant out of the bus to look behind him. The dog had stopped and just turned to walk back in the direction it had come.

'Oh, I feel awful now,' he said.

Susie seemed less concerned, 'remember what I said, he just comes and goes as he pleases.' There were hundreds of people milling about at once in all directions, so they didn't worry about being spotted and anyway most people seemed only concerned with their own movements. The ride was much shorter this time and they got off along with a few others at the corner of Baker Street and started to walk down it. It wasn't long before they saw a sign saying *The Baker Street Bazaar* and saw it was big enough to house waxwork models.

At the entrance they paid 6d to enter and were told it was an extra 6d to see the Chamber of Horrors.

'I can't believe the Chamber of Horrors is here now, isn't there enough horror here already?' whispered Susie. Jude was pensive.

'Well, what do you think, shall we go in?' he asked.

'Alright,' she said tentatively. As they walked into the darkness she asked Jude how much money he had and he said he had plenty for a full day out and evening for that matter. This had put her mind at rest, but she felt a bit cowardly in the dark and decided to walk closely behind him as they stopped and stared at the wax models. They were mostly contemporary politicians and other people that they hadn't really heard of, so couldn't compare likenesses, but the models were all quite good in their own right. One room seemed to lead into another and they walked through quietly, listening to the praises and criticisms of other visitors who knew what they were talking about. Then some people stopped in front of them and were fumbling about for money as a man stood guard outside a shrine dedicated to Napoleon.

'How much?' asked the first visitor.

'6d each, sir,' came the reply. The fee rippled down through the crowd and Jude sighed quite loudly at the extra cost but paid up. They followed others into a small area cordoned off by a wooden barrier. There didn't appear to be much there except a coach, but there was an accompanying statement from an attendant about Napoleon's attempt at escaping from Waterloo and that this was the actual coach that he had used. Suddenly the story became much more interesting and they both lingered for a while after the visitors had gone back to the mainstream exhibition.

'I wonder where the coach is now,' said Jude quietly, 'we'll have to check out Madame Tussauds when we get back.' Susie just nodded, she didn't feel comfortable discussing this with the attendant so nearby.

As they walked back to the main dark thoroughfare there was a sign pointing to the Chamber of Horrors. They went in gingerly, Susie clinging to Jude's arm; she actually thought she saw a rat scuttling into one of the corners, and wondered what on earth she was doing in a scummy place like this. Again the scene was cordoned off behind a long wooden barrier; this time the scene was incredibly gory. They walked past Robespierre and then right in front of them were the decapitated heads of Louis XVI and Marie Antoinette.

'It wouldn't surprise me if these were their actual heads,' said Susie, disgusted. She instantly thought about medieval London Bridge and how heads of traitors were impaled on pikes at the southern gatehouse for all to see, only to be tossed into the Thames to make room for others. She shuddered and focused on Jude; it was obvious he was enjoying it more. He grabbed her hand as they moved slowly along the planks of wood acting as a boardwalk. At the end was part of the original guillotiné used with fake drips of blood painted on for effect.

'I think we should leave now, it's really horrible,' said Susie. It didn't help that they were the only two visitors in there. They had to go back the way they had come in and Jude had another good look whilst Susie looked straight ahead willing the exit to appear any minute. Back in the main corridor she noticed a waxwork model of a musketeer and wandered towards it to take a closer look at the moustache on his face. She was amazed at the intricate detail on the flamboyant blouse and the large feather in his hat.

'Good day to you,' said the musketeer unexpectedly as he raised his hat.

Susie leapt back in horror; she was totally confused as he had clearly pretended to be one of the models. Instinctively she lashed out and thumped him hard in the chest; she was angry and shocked. The musketeer bent over, momentarily winded, and instead of seeing whether he was okay Jude and Susie decided to run out into the street and as far out of sight as they could, they simply couldn't afford to get into any trouble.

'What did you do that for?' asked Jude heatedly, almost out of breath.

'I couldn't help it – stupid man – he did it on purpose, he waited until I got really close to his face and then made a sharp movement to scare me out of my wits.' Her face was red with anger and embarrassment and a tear fell on to her cheek out of sheer frustration.

'Look, never mind,' said Jude looking behind him. He glimpsed someone running out of the exit and over towards a policeman. He didn't tell Susie but thought it would be best to lay low for a while, 'there's nobody coming and he probably deserved it anyway – how about we get a beer?'

'A beer, isn't it a bit early?'

'Haven't you noticed, they sell it from breakfast onwards everywhere,' he said almost pushing her into the nearest taproom. It was only ten o'clock but they had been up for ages and Susie decided to do as the locals did and had a glass of beer to shut out the world. Jude rested his glass on the table and tried to lighten the sombre mood.

'Aside from that incident, what did you think to Marie Tussauds exhibition?' he asked. Susie tried to forget about the incident and was determined to cheer up.

'Actually now that I'm out of there and don't have to go back, I thought it was quite good.'

'Yeah, me too.' Jude changed the subject, 'it feels like we've been here forever.'

'I know, I really love it here, there really is never a dull moment, talk about having to make constant rash decisions… I'm not sure about you, though, how do you feel about it?' she asked.

'I didn't really like it at first, couldn't identify with it like you obviously did, right from the start, but now I do, although I really miss everyone back home.'

'Well with any luck we'll be home before you know it, it's up to you, we could go home now you know–'

'What and miss the Great Exhibition? I'm as keen to see that as you!'

'Okay then, tomorrow morning we go.'

'Okay then,' he agreed, ruffling her hair, 'as soon as we get up.'

They left the taproom and walked back in the direction of Portland Place on the way to Hyde Park. Portland Place was rather plush, yet in nearby Norton Street Susie couldn't help notice quite a few groups of women hanging around doorways and standing in windows as if on show. She supposed it was another hazardous red light area and remembering what happened to Jude before, she didn't want to risk anything.

'There are too many women here; shall we go a different way?' she said, considerately.

Jude knew what she meant and agreed without question, but secretly thought that if they got home alright and he had any anecdotes to tell, it certainly wouldn't be that he kept running for his life away from women. They decided reluctantly to go off the beaten track towards the dreaded Tyburn, but as they strolled they became sidetracked by tiny cobbled streets interweaving with small courts and it became clear they didn't need to; eventually they came to a livelier thoroughfare which backed on to Oxford Street again. In fact they were very close to Susie's old lodgings.

'Just a minute, I want to check something.'

Jude waited whilst she went to the corner and sure enough the little dog was sitting near a bush close to the front door. She wanted to call him, but as they hadn't given him a name she just ran over to him and tapped him on his back.

'Come on, boy,' she said patting her thigh and the dog jumped up and followed loyally. Jude saw them and went to join in; he was almost as attached as Susie was. The dog's friendliness somehow made their stay here more real and the three of them stayed close as they neared the crowded streets leading to the Exhibition area where the awful stench of animals once again filled their senses.

It was Saturday and they had never seen the town so crammed or the people in such high spirits. Those in the street were parading and waving to everyone and anyone who happened to be hanging out of the windows of buildings. Jude had gauged from reading the papers here that the working classes were often blocked from joining in activities, such as library reading rooms for fear that they would ruin everything mainly from being constantly inebriated. For that reason many places closed just in time for the workers to finish their day shifts. He thought it all seemed a bit unfair but knew the rules had changed at the Great Exhibition; every citizen was given the chance to have some fun and take in the international wonders and alcohol was banned.

Perhaps that was the answer, thought Jude; places should have a Disney Park mentality. He was smirking to himself as he remembered being there with his family and his father asking for spaghetti bolognese and a beer to accompany it. A waitress dressed severely in black and white chided, 'only non-alcoholic beverages served here, sir.'

'Okay then,' said his father, 'pink lemonades all round,' as he glanced awkwardly around the room. Jude realised that Susie was trying to speak to him but he couldn't really hear now as the street volume had risen considerably; so they walked in silence, moving with the wave of people through the major streets until they finally got near to the Exhibition area where the pushing and shoving began to subside and more orderly groups descended upon the area that they knew as Kensington.

CHAPTER SIXTEEN

At the edge of Hyde Park they looked for a second time at the enormous palatial building that was made of glass. There were flags on every level at the side of the building and the semicircle of glass fanned out like a peacock at the front. It looked about three storeys high. Looking up at the glass structure they felt like mere dots in comparison. It was about lunchtime and the pale sunlight hadn't yet been taken over by the inevitable afternoon smog. The glass panels were shimmering and just inside the three large elm trees could be seen.

Susie had gleaned much of her knowledge about it from a recent visit to the Victoria and Albert Museum with some of her friends and because of this she told Jude that she would be his tour guide for the day.

'Oh, great!' he said sarcastically, but she ignored him and began in earnest.

'They built this structure around the trees to accommodate them, but they couldn't do anything about the birds flying around inside, it's a bit like an atrium.' They purchased two tickets and looked back at the little dog as they went in, who had settled under a tree. Groups of people were standing around outside the entrance and a few horse and carriages remained stationary waiting for their passengers to exit the exhibition.

Near the entrance they couldn't ignore the huge equestrian statue in front of them. People were chattering and admiring the Italian sculptor Baron Marochetti's clay monument of Richard Coeur de Lion. Susie was staring at the figure itself, the finely sculpted face, the crown upon its head, sword in right hand held high in the air and the horse in mid-gallop; she wondered whether he really did have big muscles like that, or was it artistic licence? Jude was concentrating on the grip on the reins and on the horse itself, it looked as if it was bowing down to someone. He was standing close to Susie.

'I'm guessing this is Richard the Lionheart?'

'Yes, Richard I – there should be a plinth depicting scenes from his life.' They both circled the statue but it wasn't there. 'But the statue we know of is made out of bronze.'

'That helps, I think – I knew I'd seen it, where is it now?'

'Somewhere outside the House of Lords, but it's so busy round there you can't really see the pedestal.'

They went into the main entrance area where there was a great deal to take in. A grand fountain was placed in the centre and around the sides were more statues set amongst the trees and flags. Further ahead in the distance there were forest trees and tropical plants. Looking upwards the structure was made of glass and iron in a repeating pattern. There were wooden floorboards everywhere and balconies were placed all around the edges which made it look like scaffolding, but people were walking around on all levels. One of the first things they saw was a huge lump of coal on a display stand that stated it weighed 24 tonnes.

'Apparently there are just less than two miles of exhibits, so we probably won't see them all,' said Jude, already flabbergasted.

'No, I suppose not,' agreed Susie who was distractedly looking around wondering which way to go first. Another guide was calling out to anyone who was listening as they walked past.

'All exhibits to be seen, not sold. All nations are showing the best of their kind, things of every variety.' When asked for directions to the exhibits he could be heard imparting information this way and that, 'tapestries, sir? Go to Persia,

Greece and Turkey, sir, behind Jersey, Ceylon and Malta.'

Jude and Susie headed to the Galleries. There were exhibits from all over the world. The Indian Court was assembled by the East India Company and they naturally went towards the main attraction where a large crowd had gathered around a cabinet. Inside was the Koh-i-Noor diamond, from Punjab. The information stated that it was a 105 carat diamond. It was set in a golden cage and lit up by gaslight for extra effect. There was a quiet appreciation from all who stood around it. Nearby was a model elephant with glamorously detailed and colourful embroidery on the saddle and headdress. Further round there were types of canned food and bottles of India Pale Ale, brewed in London and shipped by the East India Company.

From here they could see signs for Africa and Canada. The Canadian section was quite small and the layout was simplistic. There was maple sugar, canvases, a selection of furs and a variety of sleighs. They bypassed the Medieval Court, although it looked packed to the hilt with interesting pieces.

'Right, shall we go through the Machine Gallery now?'

'Yes, okay,' Susie replied, a little disgruntled. They probably both wanted to look at different things, but there was no way they were separating. Jude and Susie thought the Exhibition was very peaceful, although there were a few policemen, presumably to keep the crowds under control, but they were fairly redundant as there was no alcohol being served. As they passed they kept their heads low but there was so much to see they carried on in a frenzy of excitement.

'Oh my goodness, look at this,' said Susie dragging Jude over. He couldn't believe what he was seeing. The stand was labelled The Stoat Tea Party and there was a group of stuffed stoats sitting around a tea table, serving tea. In the same area there were other animals, all stuffed, one was a frog shaving his companion, and there were kittens sitting around a table also drinking tea and wearing dresses.

'This is just weird,' said Jude, not at all sure what to think, and then he noticed a bed on show and they wandered over to it.

'This is the alarm bed that Lily was talking about.' They watched someone volunteer to sit on it as part of the demonstration but he hopped off before he was thrown into the bath, much to the amusement of onlookers. Another bed was next to it.

'And look at this one, it turns into a life raft!' said Jude. Susie came over to it and they both laughed out loud at the sheer notion of needing your bed to morph into a getaway raft, but quietened down as curious bystanders regarded them warily.

'Okay, Machine Gallery?' said Jude, trying to be more serious.

'Hmm..' replied Susie, less enthused and followed him into a massive, noisy area, the clinks and banging sounds of big, loud machines all competing with each other. There were hydraulic presses, steam locomotives and hammers, an envelope folding machine which was a two person gadget to make envelopes, steam printing presses and cotton and woollen power looms in motion. A notice told them that Britain was making half of all the cotton cloth in the world. Steam filled the air, and they walked all the way through, finally going back into the main area. They walked past Sheffield hardware, including an 80-bladed penknife and a bust of Shakespeare in Portland cement. British goods were displayed everywhere, including smaller items like Coventry ribbons and Devonshire lace. By now they were losing their sense of direction. They slowed down a little and wandered over to a beautiful forty-foot model of the Liverpool docks, complete with 1600 ships. Jude was admiring the detail of the fleet when he noticed a familiar face in the crowd. He pulled Susie away from the model.

'What's the matter?' she said.

'I've just seen Lorena; I'm pretty sure she saw me but pretended she hadn't.'

'Well I thought she was our friend,' Susie said.

'Well I don't trust her, she seemed pleasant enough the other evening but I had a feeling she was just tolerating us.'

Susie had no idea he felt like this and tried to look for her. She turned round but couldn't see her, 'well I'm not leaving, there's still a lot to see and we've waited to come here; let's just walk near the edges and stay alert.'

Jude sensed her frustration and agreeing, they went into the Manufactured Goods section and found their way into the Food Hall. Although nothing was for sale it was a sight for sore eyes. The displays were spaced out well and the produce was arranged on brightly coloured cloths, the more delicate food being placed on tiered stands and covered with dome shaped glass. Some of the items making their debut were things Jude and Susie had been using for a long time – tins of condensed milk, soda water, all types of buns, imported cocoa, preserved meats, biscuits and Swiss chocolate. There were sacks of unprocessed spices, powders and grains placed around the bases of some of the stands and the aroma was a mix of cinnamon, sugar and chocolate; it was heavenly and made them both feel very hungry. They decided it was time to make their way to one of the many refreshment areas, back downstairs.

Close to part of the dining areas were signs for 'retiring rooms' and next to them were groups of people discussing the latest phenomenon, the water closet. Susie noticed the toilets first and exclaimed in glee as she hardly dared to believe it.

'Look, luxury at last!'

Jude was equally astounded and pleasantly surprised. For once they didn't have to worry about squatting in ditches. Eavesdropping further it was clear that the toilets were generally a hit with the public, although not everyone understood their purpose as some were querying the need to get washed whilst they were here; and a louder group of women sounded irritated at being charged; one of them complained.

'It says here we have to spend a penny to go, it's all very well but why aren't the men being charged?' Susie openly agreed with her but then backed away allowing them to continue their discussion. She muttered to Jude.

'She has a point, it doesn't seem fair. Hey, do you have any pennies on you; I've got to give this a go?'

Jude thought it was quite amusing and searched his pocket, bringing out a handful of pennies. By now the group of women were asking one of the official guides for an explanation.

'Don't look at me miss, it was the plumber, George Jennings, who designed and installed them and it was he who decided to charge a penny to use a cubicle, the urinals are free.'

In the cubicle further down a man was giving a demonstration of the benefits of saving water with this new toilet system. Jude drew nearer in order to listen.

'When you flush, you see,' he said flushing the toilet, 'the cistern here becomes empty and when the flush stops water can't trickle away.'

Susie returned, 'they are amazing, you are even given your own towel and someone is on hand to polish your shoes!' she could see the discussion about toilets wasn't over and didn't want to hear about them anymore, she just wanted to get something to eat but Jude couldn't get over how ingenious it was. He stood there thinking that at home the toilets seem to trickle away for ages after flushing. Somewhere along the way someone must have dispensed with the siphons, and yet all people were talking about at home was the water shortage.

'What are you thinking about?' asked Susie. She knew that

look, as though Jude had had an epiphany and was on the brink of discovering something.

'Oh nothing,' he replied, shrugging, he could hardly tell her he was wrapped up in the fascinating world of toilets, but he would look into it when he got home.

The area they chose for refreshments was set amongst trees. It was extremely busy but they found a seat at a small round table amongst mainly genteel visitors. To their surprise it was waiter service and not surprisingly they all appeared to be multilingual. They asked for the simplest items they could think of, a couple of sausage rolls, lemonade and some strawberries and pineapple. It was a while before the waiter returned, but they didn't mind as the surroundings were glorious. It was as though they were in the foyer of an enormous hotel and the outside had been brought in. Some of the trees were separated by fancy iron fencing going up and down in waves and beyond the fencing were huge palms and bright flower boxes. The glass above brought in so much light that without a breeze to spoil it they could have been on a tropical island.

Susie noticed that even the people were dressed in lighter sherbet colours. She could see lemon and lime green dresses and orange shawls and many of the men had beige coloured hats. It seemed that everyone was making the most of the occasion. Their food arrived and they paid the waiter straight away. As they ate it they listened to a conversation going on at the next table.

'You would think the food would be better than this; sausage rolls, pies, ham, jelly, do they think we don't have any taste? It's basic at best.'

'Yes,' agreed the woman, 'not very appetising is it, at least Soyer is next door, he obviously realised there would be an opportunity here.'

'Indeed, indeed,' agreed the man, 'shall we stop by at the Symposium later?'

'That would be wonderful,' she replied.

'Did you hear that?' whispered Susie to Jude, 'Soyer's Symposium – never heard of it, but it's around here somewhere'; she could hardly contain her excitement.

'Well, we'll go there later, even I'm curious now to see what all the fuss is about,' said Jude. They got up and carried on exploring the Exhibition. Finding themselves in the Eastern Dome they saw the American Department and went in, but again it was surprisingly small and snug. There were agricultural implements, a bust of Queen Victoria made out of soap, wine glasses and salt cellars plus a few stuffed squirrels and surprisingly thousands of fossils. Jude moved over to an interesting large glass cabinet. Inside was a Colt revolver which was causing a fuss because of the interchangeable mechanism. Jude, too, was fascinated; he had never seen a real gun. Next to this were rubber goods from Goodyear and a typewriter. On their way out they stopped to look at Californian opal and quartz rock.

By now they realised there was so much ground to cover they decided they would have to miss sections out; there was really far too much to see, it would probably take days; no wonder people bought season tickets. Then Jude spotted something of much interest to him. He guided Susie towards it.

'Come in here and look at this.'

The room was big and airy with far fewer people inside. They walked up to a sign that said

'Jean Bernard Léon Foucault is one of three people working on the deduction of the speed of light (measured at 186,000 miles a second). Here is his unique demonstration'. They moved to the outer edge and stood with other people who were trying to work out the mechanics of it. A long pendulum was hung from the roof which had been set to swing north and south that morning, and there was a large ring with measurements on the outside.

In the centre was a north/south dial and the pendulum was at one edge.

'What are we looking at?' asked Susie. Jude began to explain.

'As the day progresses the pendulum moves around until it swings between north east and south west. It keeps swinging in the same direction as the stars, as the earth turns beneath it, so the pendulum direction appears as though it's veering round.' Susie took a long look at it.

'Okay, think I've got you so far.'

'So this is a demonstration of the way the earth rotates,' Jude concluded.

'Oh, I see.'

'So, compared to the floor the pendulum's line of swing moves slowly clockwise, in the northern hemisphere, throughout the day.'

'Okay, now you've lost me.'

'Look,' said Jude, momentarily forgetting where he was, 'there's a more modern version of Foucault's pendulum in the Science Museum; I'll take you there some time.' Another visitor stepped forward.

'What Science Museum, where? I've never heard of it – who are you? It was very interesting what you were saying.'

'I told you,' said another voice and Lorena stood out from behind him looking pointedly at Jude, 'it is you, isn't it? I've been watching you; you're the people the police are looking for – and to think you came to our house for dinner; your behaviour was distasteful at best – I've got to find my father, he's here somewhere.'

Jude panicked, 'no, no, honestly, it's not us–'

Lorena didn't tarry, she hurried towards the door and out into the walkway, but Jude was quick on her tail and caught her by the arm, swinging her round.

'What are you going to do?' he asked.

'Why, inform my father of course, he thinks you are master counterfeiters and he's got the whole town looking for you.' Jude thought quickly.

'And who's that you are with?'

Lorena looked concerned, 'why do you ask?'

'Well, are you supposed to be with him or are you sneaking around? I hear the Exhibition is a great place for clandestine get-togethers.' Lorena's expression changed from concern to embarrassment.

'What does it have to do with you?'

'I won't tell your father if you won't,' said Jude. At that point Lorena's escort was at her side, followed closely by Susie.

'What's going on?' he asked.

'Nothing, I was mistaken,' replied Lorena, shrugging and staring at her feet.

The man had had enough of this silliness, 'well come on, we don't have much time left.'

'Yes, yes of course,' said Lorena, walking off as if nothing had happened.

'Not sure what you said, but it must have been good,' said Susie.

'I'll tell you over that French dinner,' said Jude more calmly than he felt. He had been bluffing – he actually had no idea whether this was a place for a secret rendezvous.

They passed the Chinese section and through the open gap could see Chinese lanterns hanging from the ceiling and against a red background were paintings of Chinese art hanging on the walls and huge blue and white chintz urns placed around the sides. But they were slightly distracted now so Susie suggested they made their way to the Soap and Perfumery section, thinking that the scents might lessen their anxiety.

Jude noticed that there were seven hundred exhibitors there and sighed.

'Don't worry, we'll whistle through in no time,' said Susie and held his forearm to lead him through the thickest part of the surging visitors. The pleasant smell of mixed bouquets hung in the air and there was another selection of celebrity soaps; one in the form of a contemporary singer. There was even a fountain overflowing with eau-de-cologne which gave off a strong, but flowery scent for a few yards around it. As promised, Susie didn't linger and they found themselves in the British half of the exhibition. Here there was too much to see; military arms, chemicals, examples of civil engineering, glass chandeliers, pottery, medical instruments and musical instruments, including a four-person piano. Drawing a lot of attention was a remarkable wedding cake of brass locks, about three feet high. Each lock could be opened individually but one Bramah key at the top could lock all of them simultaneously. There was also a Chubb recording lock which informed the owner if anyone had tried to pick it, but one item stood out for Susie who marched over to it, with Jude following quickly behind.

'This is a bit strange,' she said. They were surrounded by artefacts, amazing pieces demonstrating the excellent skills of silversmiths and in particular she was focusing on a gigantic Lambert and Rawlings flagon.

'I've seen this at the V&A Museum recently.'

'Have you?'

'Yes, it stood out then.' She stepped closer, 'look at it – what a huge piece of silver; I recognise the parcel-gilt edging and the large chain that connects to the lid.' Jude looked at it; it was rather amazing, huge and rich in detail rivalling the other extraordinary works of art they had seen.

'I wonder whether, over the years, it has hardly moved from this spot.'

'I've no idea, but I'm guessing probably not,' said Susie, thinking that every time she saw something familiar it had the adverse effect on her; instead of feeling comforted she felt more insecure about ever returning home.

She shook the feeling off and they went over to the other side where there was much more to see including toys and fishing materials and a spacious stained glass area which was more sectioned off and quieter. It was here that they decided to make this their last stop; they needed to slow down. They sat on a bench looking at the large pieces of rectangle and oval shaped glass with their different patterns and colours. This quieter area was a welcome reprieve from the crowds and they found a bench almost hidden around a corner. They sat for a while, both feeling uncertain at the way events were unfolding after the incident with Lorena and both now unsure about their chances of getting home. Susie sighed and rested her head against Jude's shoulder. He put his arm around her tightly and for no reason at all their hug turned into a kiss. Then they sat for a while just staring at the glass and contemplating the emotional ups and downs of the journey which had so worn them out, yet brought them closer together. They kissed again; more passionately this time before getting up hand in hand and heading towards the exit.

They were almost outside when Susie saw something out of the corner of her eye, quickly catching her attention. Another sign over on the right hand side said '*for the future*'. She walked over to the glass cabinet. There were only a few people standing around it.

'Oh no,' she gasped loudly. Jude was a few steps behind her, 'what's wrong?'

'Look,' she whispered, pointing. Jude didn't go any further. He got close to the cabinet and peered over the heads of the people in front of him and saw placed carefully in a bright display Susie's charms, her zip and his watch. He hardly dare move and slowly scouted the area around him. He could see a policeman standing in the corner watching them carefully. He thought it was strange that a display such as this wasn't put in a more prominent position and assumed it had only been put there to trap them. He stepped backwards, putting his arm around Susie's waist and told her to do the same.

'Don't look worried or surprised, now let's walk forwards and you start chatting to me casually, I'll just nod in agreement as we look at the objects on the way out.' Susie did as he suggested but couldn't help looking back at the policeman, who was listening to Calvin's father talking to him animatedly. He looked up and saw her, but she quickened her pace.

'Come on,' she said to Jude in a panic as she saw the policeman begin to move at a steady pace in their direction. Wasting no time, Jude and Susie's walk turned into a dash, dodging through the crowds to break them up, making it harder for them to be reached, weaving their way towards the left hand side of the exit. Once outside they ran between the carriages, eventually reaching a line of trees, where they stopped to catch their breath. They stayed there until they were sure it was clear. In the distance they had watched the policeman and a few others charge out, look around in all directions, meet up again and finally venture back into the Exhibition.

'This is all too close for comfort. I'm scared now; we can't afford to get caught. What should we do?' Susie asked.

'I think we should still go to Soyer's, it's the last place they'll look for us; we could be a mile away by now,' replied Jude. Susie was uncertain, so Jude placed both his hands on her shoulders.

'Look – not everybody's searching for us and not everyone would have read the papers, we will have to keep it in perspective,' he reasoned. By now the natural light was starting to fade and dusk was approaching. This time they knew they would feel safer the darker it got. 'Okay,' she said; not sure what other choice they had.

CHAPTER SEVENTEEN

Emerging from the trees they found themselves in the gardens of Gore House. They both stared at a sign which read:

Soyer's Symposium, Gore House, Kensington
(The Residence of the late Countess of Blessington)
Nearly Opposite the Crystal Palace
Gigantic Dining Encampment of All Nations – 400 feet long,
The largest Dining Room in the world
French-English Dinner – 2s each
In the Baronial Hall – Dinner, Anglo-Francais – 3s 6d
In the Mansion, 4 continental Tables D'Hote à la Francaise daily –
6s 6d

'Well – we knew it wouldn't be far away, hard to miss it,' said Susie looking around, she could already see a statuary and knew they must be in for some surprises. She looked back at the sign, 'I think we've missed the 2 shilling dinner, that was this afternoon, anyway let's decide when we've checked it all out – look at this beautiful landscaped garden and these statues.' She wandered towards them. Jude looked behind him just to make sure they hadn't been followed. It looked clear. As he caught up with her he tried to imagine where all these dining areas were.

'I suppose I shouldn't be surprised that there's more than one choice,' he said.

'Yes, I've been trying to work it out. It looks like outside there's the Baronial Banqueting Hall and then there's a much larger marquee called The Encampment of All Nations which seats over a thousand people, or you can dine inside the mansion itself. She was keen to see the mansion so they went there first. Jude paid the admission and they went up the steps into Gore House. Inside the air was filled with an exotic fragrance emanating from all the plants.

'Look,' said Jude, 'he's even got a Hall of Architectural Wonders.' They didn't go in but as they passed they could see replicas of the Bridge of Sighs and the Leaning Tower of Pisa. They continued on and saw a Grecian Temple called La Salle du Parnasse. Greek urns were placed around the sides and white material was draped around gold pillars. They watched guests go inside exclaiming how large the room was and being informed that it used to be the old library. They decided to try the chamber called La Forêt Péruvienne and were each given a glass of iced champagne as they entered. Apparently the room was designed to resemble a South American Rainforest at night as the scene was hazy and moonlit. Real palm trees were set amongst the moon and stars and there was even a tropical breeze. They stayed there for a while whilst they finished their champagne.

Across the way they went into a much larger, brighter room, La Salle de Noces de Danaë. Around the walls and cascading from the ceiling were hundreds of gold and silver teardrops which were set against a bright green and gold chequered ceiling from which globes of shimmering glass hung down. By now they were speechless at the flamboyancy and care in the details and they moved up to the first floor; even the walls around the staircase were painted with a combination of people and animals. At the top they passed a French themed corridor where cupids were hung in the air as if in flight and then saw another room, The Grotte des Neiges Éternelles which they couldn't resist.

'This is unbelievable,' said Jude. They were looking up at the overhanging stalactites, 'how on earth did they make all these icicles, I thought freezing hadn't really begun yet.' Susie agreed, although she had already seen the beginnings of it with the ice cream vendor. To her right she could see an animal; she was startled at first until she realised it wasn't real, 'look at that Arctic fox, what a gorgeous colour; but it's stuffed like everything else around here,' she said, looking dejected.

Jude wasn't sure what to say, he was surprised at the disdain in her voice; by now he supposed she wouldn't be shocked by anything. Anyway there wasn't much they could do about it. More drinks were being offered, so they accepted. They noticed that in each room there were chairs and tables with plates and cutlery so that people could linger over small buffets in order to stay longer and marvel over the wonders. The rooms weren't crowded, either, and all in all they couldn't believe what an extraordinary time they were having. Susie noticed a fragrant smell of roses in the room, but couldn't understand where it was coming from, although it seemed to be from above. After a while the effects from the cold rooms were beginning to make her shiver so she persuaded Jude to go into a warmer room, and they chose the Italian Palazzo next. Inside were murals of Calabrian landscapes, models of classical ruins and a really large vine climbing up one wall full with wax grapes drooping down. There was more to see but by now Jude was getting hungry so they went on to a terrace and down some stairs that led to the back garden. Tucked under the stairs was an open air American Cocktail Bar, which they both couldn't resist going into.

Jude was still scanning the groups of people standing around; he found it difficult to relax, having assured Susie that they would be fine here. However, Susie's excitement was rubbing off on him and he felt privileged to visit two cocktail bars in one week and, looking at the board, this one certainly had the edge where choice was concerned. The list of drinks varied from brandy smashes and sherry cobblers to Tongue

Twisters, Knockemdowns, Squeezemtights and for the first time Susie noticed Soyer's own Nectars on display. Some of the men were smoking cigars but refreshingly they could see women moving freely amongst them, clearly enjoying themselves. They chose their drinks, Jude thought he would try a Tongue Twister and Susie chose champagne but with one of Soyer's Nectars mixed in. It was blue in colour and tasted of lemon and cinnamon.

'Do you realise that this is just about where the Royal Albert Hall stands?' she said.

'Really?' Jude was uncertain and tried to look around for something familiar so he could get his bearings.

'Yes,' she replied, wondering how she could persuade him, 'did you see the sign on the way in for music newly arrived in London, some kind of harmonic orchestra, maybe this was where the idea for a music venue came from.'

'Maybe,' replied Jude, tentatively. In the distance they could see that a theatrical show was about to begin, and lanterns were balanced in some of the trees creating unusual displays of light.

Susie had heard of the Grotto of Ondine and was keen to go and explore, so they left the bar.

'Come and look at this,' she said coaxing Jude in the direction of a small pavilion. They hovered outside for a while watching the water cascade down from the top, to try and gauge how quickly to jump through without getting soaked by the spray, But inside it was delightful. The ceiling comprised of crystals and gold and silver fish made out of a shiny material were moving around.

'How back to front, having fish above us,' said Jude.

'Somehow it doesn't surprise me at all.' Susie was looking at the top where a statuette of Hebe was holding a cup of nectar from which real liqueurs were coming down through different chutes. Jude pointed out the statue of Ondine to her while he picked up an empty glass for them both. Some of the guests were moving quickly away, laughing and not wanting to get wet from the liqueurs or the water behind them.

Jude saw the statue suddenly move before Susie, 'careful,' he said, 'it was a statue and now it's not, it's moving – promise me you're not going to go over and punch it in the chest.' Susie had already seen it and dug him in the ribs with her elbow, 'very funny.' She watched the statue taking glasses off people and filling them with liqueurs. They tried drinks from a couple of the chutes and not surprisingly all of them were different flavours. 'What a novelty,' said Jude, trying a third. Susie, though, was ready to discover more. Close by she could see that some of Soyer's Magic Stoves were on display, some were being purchased, and so they finished their drinks and went to take a closer look. It appeared they had just missed a demonstration but on closer inspection the stove was quite small and looked like it was made of two parts; a copper pot and an adjacent lantern where presumably the methylated spirit was vaporised and lit.

Susie was enthused again, 'this is meant to be used as a portable, table top stove. Soyer invented quite a few gadgets; he was even associated with using one of the first gas ovens: in fact we saw one in the Exhibition, actually they didn't appear for years after that, I wonder why?'

Jude didn't really know either, 'Perhaps people were afraid of gas explosions, or maybe there wasn't any provision for gas, it's a bit like us not moving on from using petrol, it takes a while for things to change.' Susie shrugged and they carried on walking until they reached the Baronial Hall. They could see the marquee was made of imitation stone in the style of a castle and the roof panelling was similar to that at the Exhibition, a mixture of glass and iron in repeating patterns. The tables were set out in the shape of a horseshoe and there was a separate area hidden away for the musicians. It was certainly homely; the walls were draped with material and there were statuettes and hundreds of oil paintings gracing the walls and the marquee was very well lit, but they decided to go for the cheaper option of the Encampment, which was also much larger so they could blend in with the crowds of diners more easily.

Having no idea where it was they had to ask one of the members of staff, 'you walk across the Pré d' Orsay and it is at the far end.' It was quite a walk to reach it, across a kind of meadow, but they just followed the smell of roast beef that encircled the area around the Encampment and soon came upon the outside kitchen. Inside they couldn't help but notice an enormous dining table in the centre of the room and they waited to be seated somewhere along it. It didn't take long and the sights and smells of the roast dinners wafting straight past them made them ravenous. They knew they wouldn't go hungry here. All types of roast could be seen; roast beef and ox, saddle of lamb, legs of mutton, small chickens, roast pork with sage and onion and Symposium pies were placed on the table along with spinach, peas and sprouts and they hurriedly tucked in.

Susie looked up to see a man cruising around the table. He was wearing a cape and his trademark red beret and she knew at once it was Alexis Soyer. She could hear him speaking to some people at the table next to theirs.

'Yes, madam, you are correct it is not all spinach,' he picked up a nearby dish, 'these are nettles; they look the same but that is why you say they are peppery.' The woman was nodding and saying something that Susie couldn't hear. Soyer nodded in agreement, 'Yes, indeed, just because they grow freely it is common to think they are less nourishing – but it is to the contrary and it is the same with watercress, thank you Madam; enjoy.'

Before long he was standing beside Susie and her heart skipped a beat.

'Hello my good friends, I see you are 'ungry, I hope you are enjoying zis display of food, eh? – if you notice we are not using the roasting spit; all food is roasted in our big ovens.'

Susie had already seen the rows of brick and metal gas ovens being operated by chefs who were intent on giving them their full attention. She knew that Soyer had acquired a taste for English food and, unlike other French chefs, had no qualms about providing roast dinners to the public. She was lost for words, so Jude stepped in.

'Er, yes, we were just wondering how you managed to use a gas oven in the Reform Club.' Soyer simply smiled.

'Well it was easy; you see the gas was already in place in Pall Mall.' He looked around to check that his other guests were happy enough. Susie instantly lost her shyness and her enthusiasm kicked in.

'Hello Alexis, my name is Susanna.' She paused for a moment and then lowered her voice, 'I just think you are remarkable.' She got up and pushed her chair back to meet him face to face.

'I hope everyone appreciates what you do; the soup kitchens you created–' there was a slight pause, 'your aspiration to simply show everyone how to cook, and your inventions – your vegetable strainer is like a watering can – brilliant.' Jude shuffled awkwardly, but she hadn't finished, 'and we are still using your kitchen timer…. they should have made a statue out of you.' She felt a nudge from Jude. Soyer had been regarding her curiously, but didn't seem to think her comments were out of hand. He took her hand and kissed it whilst he thanked her for her generous compliments, before moving to the next group of people. Susie sat down again and was quiet, she was star struck and felt flabbergasted that he had walked over and talked to them.

'That was a bit of an outburst wasn't it? I thought people only got like that about rock stars!' Susie still felt captivated but was now a little embarrassed and had another sip of wine. She pulled her chair up close to Jude's, checking that no one could hear.

'That's not the end of it. He gives all this up soon and goes to the Crimea with his stove and gridiron to allow the army to be catered for instead of them having to cook for themselves.'

Jude glanced up and watched Soyer circulate amongst his guests.

'How did that come about?' he asked.

'It was a request from a British soldier who asked him for some simple recipes,' she replied.

'It shows how well-regarded he must have been then,' said Jude who by now was also regarding him as something of an enigma.

Susie watched Jude as he contemplated the whole episode; he was finding it surreal that he had communicated directly with a pioneer from the past. His eyes met Susie's and they exchanged a look of mutual understanding; she was so glad to have him around and squeezed his leg under the table. They finished their food and sat taking in the busy scene of a thousand or so diners and waiters walking up and down laden with trays and then decided to leave.

CHAPTER EIGHTEEN

As they left the Hyde Park area Susie suddenly remembered something.

'We've forgotten about the little dog, oh I feel awful, we just left him,' she said in disbelief at them both. Jude had also completely forgotten about him.

'Look, let's be rational, it wasn't our fault, we were practically chased out of the Exhibition. Anyway he's been here a lot longer than us. He'll find someone else, and he knows how to live off the street – at least he seems free of the trainer now.'

Susie was thoughtful, 'I wonder why he chose us?'

'I've been thinking about it too – maybe we smell different – I don't know about you but he kept sniffing my shoes all the time; I know that dogs can even detect disease just by sniffing – maybe our scents stand out a mile from everyone here – he seemed to be able to match us two up anyhow.'

'That's true,' said Susie. He was right, there was no point in dwelling on it and unable to resist, they decided to take the last chance to experience the London nightlife together. They walked straight towards Piccadilly. It was just before ten o'clock and the shops were beginning to close. There were still a few street vendors around, mostly men selling stationery and knives and elderly women trying to shift the last of their fruit and flowers.

'I'm a bit short of money, I'd feel better if I pawned this silk tie,' said Jude fumbling with the cloth around his neck.

'I'm not sure, how about we change it for a cotton one and keep the difference. I think you'll need a tie if we're going into the saloons.'

'Okay, but you go in on your own and I'll wait out here, we shouldn't be seen together.' Susie looked worried, but Jude placated her.

'It's okay, they're looking for silver, not silk.'

As it happened there were only a handful of people inside and the pawnbroker seemed distracted, probably waiting to close. He hardly took any notice of Susie as she pointed to a cotton handkerchief, exchanged it with the silk and quickly took the change he had given her and left.

Her instincts were right, around the streets the dress code seemed to have changed. Gone was the casual day wear, instead vibrant and fancy costumes were being paraded around. Many of the men were wearing fine silk accessories and most of the women were in decorative dresses set out in extravagant colourful layers. A few well-dressed children accompanied their parents, but conversely, running in and out of alleyways other youngsters could be seen wearing dowdy rags, occasionally going up to people on the main street and singing to them, and asking for money in return. The poorer groups of men and women could always be seen but tonight seemed outnumbered by the glittering throngs of theatre and party goers and the atmosphere was decidedly convivial and jolly.

Jude and Susie had seen a tavern tucked away on a side street which had an adjacent small music hall attached. They were intrigued by the boozy sounds of singing as they approached the open doorway. This was a new experience for them. They went to the bar which was quite basic with wooden low bar stools, some of which were slightly broken and splintered. They ordered a couple of small glasses of pale ale and perched on two better stools that appeared to be isolated, neither belonging to a table or the bar and were facing the stage. The woman who was entertaining appeared a little rough at the edges, with sleeves rolled up and had an aggressive expression on her face whilst she sang her song.

'Can you work out what she's singing about?' asked Susie.

'Not sure, something about the drunkards and the dispossessed…it makes you realise that these people are not indifferent to their predicament – she's really angry at the unfairness of her situation.'

The song was outrageously rude and the singer was clearly hostile. Then a man came up on to the stage, and the tone only got worse. He also sang about his gloomy life but went on to humiliate the opposite sex in the process.

The foul language reminded Susie of her night in Covent Garden. 'The words are similar, but the attitude is definitely more sinister,' she told Jude as they watched the audience swaying in their seats, singing along; the men shaking their fists and the women hitching their dresses up and parading round with a look of defiance. They had soon had enough, quickly realising that this wasn't the kind of evening they had anticipated and went back to join the jollity in the streets.

As they walked towards the Haymarket a few omnibuses passed them but most people out for the evening were also on foot. Again the atmosphere reminded Susie of being on holiday when everyone strolls along the promenade just taking in the sights and sounds. At the top of the Haymarket traffic began to fill the streets and stepping from carriages were men from the Army and Navy and others in velveteen trousers, possibly here for the weekend. They passed numerous French restaurants, oyster shops, hotels and coffee houses. The theatres were emptying and people began scurrying into the next entertainment areas already lined up. They were on Great Windmill Street where the brightest gin palaces stood out; but then Susie noticed a huge casino near the café Riche – it was the Argyll Rooms.

'We've got to go in here, I've heard so much about this place,' she said taking Jude's hand and guiding him in. He hesitated at the entrance.

'I don't think we should gamble, I can't chance the money we've got left.'

'It's not a casino in that sense, it's what they call a large saloon bar with a dance floor,' Susie replied excitedly. They paid a shilling to get in.

'Did you notice some of the women on the streets passing their business cards to the men?' asked Susie as they walked down a narrow corridor.

'Yeah, you couldn't help but notice.'

'Well this venue is just an extension of that but in an upper class way.'

'Oh, okay, I suppose there's no getting away from it,' replied Jude by now realising the extent of the predicament for women and that this was just the accepted status quo around here.

Nevertheless, inside it was huge and glamorous and no doubt a premier dance saloon. There were pristine aristocrats, uniformed gentlemen and men in regular suits mingling together with pretty courtesans wearing bold satin and silk dresses. The bright lights combined with mirrored walls and ceilings and extravagant red and gold drapes and ornaments made it feel glitzy and exhilarating. The band was lively and the dancing even livelier and they stood on the outskirts watching for some time. They eventually paid the extra to go to the upstairs gallery and bar and sat on velvet benches sipping red wine and carried on watching the dancing below, having decided to stay out of the public glare. All too soon the place began to empty and they could hear people asking if it was twelve o'clock already and discussing where they were going to go next.

Jude and Susie filtered out en masse with everyone else and decided to go to a coffee house. They sat near a window and ordered coffee whilst watching the people outside going by. Already voices in the street were becoming more raucous and behaviour in general was becoming more loose and carefree. The coffee house was busy and they noticed a couple of official looking men cross the street and approach the door. Suddenly the loud noise of clinking glasses and decanters could be heard as they were scooped up and passed quickly into a back room and in exchange more coffee was speedily passed around the tables. The men came in, totally unaware of the mad dash to clear the tables, sat down and ordered coffees. Whilst they were being poured the men could be seen scanning the room. Jude and Susie assumed they were looking for them and bowed their heads low in conversation. About ten minutes went by and the men got up to leave. Jude and Susie breathed a sigh of relief but then so did the rest of the occupants who whistled and cheered softly. The brandy and glasses were brought straight back out and conversations continued heartily.

'We've got to stop being paranoid,' said Jude, 'that wasn't about us at all, maybe this place is unlicensed or something.' Susie didn't really know, but her thoughts were elsewhere.

'I was thinking, do you think anyone will believe us back home?'

'Believe what?' said Jude, who by now was feeling quite tense.

'Well all of it. I can hardly believe what I'm seeing myself half the time. Sometimes I think I'm just dreaming, but then everything's so loud and larger than life that you just get wrapped up in it.' Jude sighed.

'I know what you mean – if I was here on my own I would think it was here that I lived and my other world was a distant dream.'

'But you're not, we're here together.'

They clasped each other's hands tight across the table.

'Well,' said Jude, 'do you want to go back or shall we go somewhere else?'

'Go back where?' she replied.

'Good point, all the hotels and lodging houses will probably be alerted – the only suggestion I can think of is Calvin's chambers.'

'But what about Lily, she'll probably be the first to give us away?'

'We don't know that, anyway let's worry about that when we get there,' said Jude, who suddenly felt a desperate need to be somewhere safe.

Outside the scene had changed dramatically. It was now the early hours of the morning, yet the streets were still quite lively. Certain doorways had brightly lit gas lamps above them and people were notably disappearing into them even though at first sight they looked like they belonged to residents. Susie noticed more and more people were stumbling around in the street; a few just stopped in their tracks and were sitting around on kerbsides or steps shouting obscenities. There were quite a few policemen circulating quickly trying to move them on. Realising they would soon be in the centre of the trouble brewing, they dodged quickly out of the way, finding the nearest place to escape to until the disorder died down.

'Let's go in here,' said Jude pointing to the nearest lit up doorway. On the other side of the door they were asked to pay. Further inside there was a surprisingly large saloon, smaller than the Argyll Rooms but set out in a similar layout. The atmosphere was warm and friendly and everyone was clearly enjoying themselves, many of them elegantly dressed, presumably on their next round after the larger saloons had closed. They found a couple of seats and watched the dancers glide across the room. Jude became more relaxed.

'What a surprise I thought it was going to be a tiny Bistro or something.'

'Do you know how the word Bistro got its name?' asked Susie who always enjoyed these conundrums.

'Tell me what you think first and then I'll tell you what I think,' said Jude playing her at her own game.

'Well, when the Russians took over Paris earlier this century they went into little cafés saying "Bystro, Bystro" to the waiters who were keeping them waiting.'

'And?' queried Jude.

'In Russian Bistro means faster – hence "Faster, Faster".'

'How strange for that to stick if it is true,' said Jude. 'I heard that the bistro came a bit later and that it comes from the word bistrouille, a combination of brandy and coffee, more apt I would have thought; at least its connected to drinks found in a café.'

'Oh–' Susie replied, confused, 'that's the trouble with these things, for every one explanation there will always be someone who contends it.'

'Come on,' said Jude impulsively, 'let's dance.' Susie needed no persuasion and couldn't believe her luck that he had even suggested it. They joined in with the dancers, half doing their own thing and half trying to keep up with the moves and stayed on the floor for at least half an hour before becoming purposefully wedged together. Not wanting to part, eventually they went upstairs and asked for soft drinks to quench their thirst and drank them almost at once.

'I really miss water,' said Jude.

'Yeah, so do I – I think I saw some bottled at the Exhibition but for some reason I still didn't trust it,' said Susie, yawning.

'I think it's time to go, don't you?'

She nodded, but I do really like the atmosphere in here, I wish we had found this place earlier, there's nothing like it back at home.'

'Well, I suppose we have nightclubs.'

'I know, but somehow it's not the same.' Susie wasn't sure how she felt about anything anymore and knew she was overtired.

When they came out the street scene had deteriorated even more. Gone were the neatly dressed gentlemen with their polished leather boots and the gracious women who accompanied them and left were drunken men and women, half-dressed, rolling around in the street. They had to step over one woman who seemed out cold and had completely blocked their path. Her hat was nowhere to be seen. There were shouts and screams in the distance and they saw people in front of them being blatantly robbed. Susie felt the men leering at her as she walked past and one clutched at her wrist; she shook it free saying to Jude 'for heaven's sake, let's get out of here.' They walked to the nearest cab stand and shook the driver hard to wake him up. They got in and asked to go directly to Grosvenor Square. As they rode out they saw another woman collapse in the street and two policemen come to her aid with a stretcher. Even though they felt relatively safe, their ankles were locked together as if they were bracing themselves for the cab to suddenly take flight. After witnessing the cab driver dodging a minefield of groups of shouting and swearing men and women, threatening behaviour gradually vanished into the distance and they sat in peace for the rest of the ride.

'Well, we did choose to come to the liveliest spot at the worst time of day,' said Jude with a smile. 'Don't you mean night?' said Susie, her sense of humour returning.

In the end they asked the cab driver to stop before Grosvenor began. They needed fresh air and didn't want to get too close for fear of being watched. As they walked through the echoing streets it was clear that most people by now were asleep. When they approached Calvin's residence they both paused.

'It's not worth knocking at the door, we don't want to disturb Lily,' said Jude.

'What do you suggest?'

Jude looked upwards, he knew which room was Calvin's

from the inside, but it was harder to make out from the outside. He settled on the long window in the middle on the second floor.

'I'm going to throw some stones at the window and try and wake him, you look out for any movement.' Susie stood quietly and watched while he picked some light gravel-like stones sending them scattering across the window to imitate the sound of hard rain. They stood back and watched – nothing. He picked up another handful and tossed them more directly at the window. Susie saw a curtain move and some ruffled hair appear at the window. 'Someone's heard,' she whispered. They quickly mounted the steps to the front door and waited either side of it, in case the wrong person answered and they needed a quick getaway. To their relief it was Calvin.

'What are you doing here?' he said, looking both pleased and worried.

'Sorry, Calvin, we didn't know where else to go; we're going home tomorrow. Could we stay here tonight?'

'Come in, quickly,' he said, putting his head outside once they had entered to check that no one had followed them.

'The chamber is free upstairs and you can have the room next to mine on the second floor,' he said looking at Susie. They went quietly up the stairs and when they reached the second floor Susie said nothing and silently went into the room that Calvin had suggested. Calvin looked at Jude.

'My father is very angry, you know, he thinks you are both experienced counterfeiters or tricksters and wants you locked up as soon as possible. I think he is worried that you are going to incriminate me, somehow.'

'We are nothing of the sort – we're not from around here, but those silver charms do belong to us, or did, I should say, we brought them with us.'

Calvin looked incredulous, 'brought them with you from where?'

Jude glanced down at the floor.

'Look,' said Calvin, 'get some sleep, I will wake you in a couple of hours – and don't go down. I don't want Lily to know you are here – she suspected there was something different about you from the start.' With that he went back into his own room and Jude went up the next level of stairs and got straight into bed.

CHAPTER NINETEEN

It could only have been a few hours later when Susie woke from a deep sleep to the sound of a dawn chorus from birds sat in a tree outside her window. She could see daylight glimpsing through the gaps in the curtains but had no idea what the time was. She sat up, alert and looked around the room. It was a peaceful room; the walls were decorated in cream leaf-patterned wallpaper and the drapes were a gold colour. She sat back against the pillow and looked at the matching bedcovers and thought how she would love to have a room of her own like this. She fleetingly wished that she hadn't woken so early but was now aware of a knot in her stomach, caused from apprehension rather than hunger. Most of her clothes were thrown over a small rococo chair in the corner. She got out of bed and put them on, gathered the rest of her things and left the room. She went straight up the stairs to Jude's quarters and found him in a deep sleep. The room was still quite dark and not wanting to alarm him she sat on the bed next to him and whispered his name. With no response she resorted to pushing him over on to his other side. He awoke with a start, but she quickly put her fingers to his lips to quieten him.

'It's pretty early, I know, but I think we should get going,' she said. Hardly awake Jude began putting on the clothes he had discarded, by which time Susie was beginning to pace up and down.

'Should we wake Calvin or should we just go?' she asked. Jude hesitated for a moment. 'Let's go.'

They moved quickly down the stairs and were in the hall trying to open the front door when Lily approached them from the kitchen. She was obviously startled to see Susanna and a gratifying look of acknowledgement swept across her face. Within moments a young man they hadn't met before was by her side. Jude and Susie felt a temporary paralysis, but tried to calmly explain their way out. Lily nudged the young man, who went straight out the front door and she looked at them both questioningly.

'Well, the audacity – turning up here. I've seen your forged coin, you know, have you stolen anything from the house on your way out? In a bit of a hurry aren't you? Wait here while I go and fetch Calvin.' She hoisted up her skirts and marched up the flights of stairs. They waited until she was out of sight and then opened the front door but quickly shut it again when they saw the young man returning with a policeman beside him. Seconds later the door was pushed open and the two gentlemen came in and they all stood together in the hall.

'I think you need to come with me,' said the policeman to Jude and Susanna.

But Calvin came rushing down the stairs; his clothes had been hurriedly put on and were all adrift. He was holding on to the bannister and almost leapt over the last four steps to the ground.

'Leave them alone, they are my guests,' he said, slightly out of breath.

'I've got orders, sir,' replied the policeman, 'and these two people fit the descriptions nicely.'

'Alright – give me a moment, I want to have a word with them in here.' The policeman nodded and Calvin took them into a room towards the back of the house.

Inside he turned to them pleadingly, 'Who are you really? – I don't like to be disloyal to my father but I consider you my friends and am very disheartened.'

Jude decided it was time to be honest and was about to speak but Calvin had remembered something.

'I've been meaning to ask – why do you have my name embroidered on your strange undergarment, if you can call it that, I've never seen anything like it?'

Jude was taken aback, he hadn't thought of that, but then he wasn't expecting his clothes to be rummaged through while he slept. As if reading his thoughts Calvin added, 'Lily told me.'

'Look, you've been a great friend – if we tell you the truth I'm afraid you won't believe us,' said Jude.

'Go on,' replied Calvin, adamant to hear the truth. Jude glanced at Susie.

'Where we come from clothes designers sometimes have their name sewn into garments, it's a way of advertising.'

'And where do you come from exactly?' asked Calvin.

'We're from the future,' Jude replied, he could see Calvin's eyebrows rise but he carried on.

'We fell through a hedgerow, literally, it wasn't intended. We were at college, just about to have a coffee break.' Jude's words were languishing hopelessly; he was beginning to realise how absurd it all sounded. He looked again at Susie, who decided to continue.

'If you are looking for proof we can tell you things that there is no way we would know – we can tell you things that will happen decades from now.' As Calvin said nothing, she thought she would go for it.

'There will be two more outbreaks of cholera, the last being in 1864; by then there will be control over the sewerage system. They will begin building an underground railway system – steam trains will go through at first, but eventually a sophisticated underground network will cover the whole of London.' Jude got the knack of what she was trying to do and interrupted.

'Football will have rules and a Football Association will be set up. It will become a national game with teams all over the

British Isles taking part, it's still one of the best loved games and it will take off when companies begin to close earlier on Saturdays.'

Calvin was attentive, 'Well then – exactly when in the future are you from?'

'The twenty-first century.'

Calvin laughed, 'I want to believe you, I really do, and I suppose time will only tell if what you say is true–' He liked these people and didn't believe they had done anything wrong, obviously the story about the future was a little far-fetched; their only fault was to hide the truth of their real whereabouts and how they came by the unusual silver ornaments for fear of exactly this; being hounded like dogs by the police.

Calvin thought about how furious his father would be, but he had made his decision and walked over to the large sash window.

'Listen, we will go out this way.'

'What?' Susie gasped looking down below, but Calvin ignored her.

'Jude you go first, hold on to the ivy and use it to lower yourself down. Susanna, you go next.'

Without hesitation she followed Jude and climbed backwards out of the window. She slipped straight away, her face catching the branch of a nearby tree that was jutting out; she knew she had scratched it badly, her face stung immediately. She was shocked but the adrenaline kept her going. Jude was waiting at the bottom ready to catch her if she fell and she could see Calvin's boots just above her head. She jumped to the ground.

'Oh, no, your face is bleeding,' said Jude, who went and found a large leaf and placed it on her cheek, 'keep it there to keep the pressure on to stop the flow of blood.' He looked past her at Calvin who was in a hurry.

'Right, this way, we will go straight through the gardens

and yards and then finally under an archway; I'll wait for you there.' It was obvious he had done this before, thought Jude as they tried to keep up with him; it was difficult because the smell of the cesspits was so bad they had to pinch their noses with one hand. After the third garden they had lost him, but then Susie saw an archway almost hidden in one corner and they went through. There was a final small yard which led out on to the pavement where Calvin was standing.

'We will wait for a passing carriage over there on that corner.' They crossed the road with him and they stood waiting for what seemed like ages.

'Where do you need to go?' enquired Calvin.

'I'm not sure entirely but we came in on the outskirts of the town and then it was a short walk towards a clothes market – I can't remember the name – but it was near the Tower, I think,' replied Jude.

'If you're talking about the Rag Fair, that's miles – look I'll come with you,' said Calvin.

Susie couldn't speak; her nerves had got the better of her. In the distance she could see two policemen quite far apart but signalling towards each other, but a carriage was on its way and Calvin stopped it, told the driver he would be paid on his return and they all got in.

They all remained still; not quite believing what had just happened and not daring to speak. Susie thought how quiet the streets were but then remembered that it was Sunday again. The carriage took them on to Oxford Street, following quite a direct route towards Holborn. Jude was amazed that they had managed to be here for a whole week and had avoided going near to Newgate prison. It was a choice they had purposefully made but now he wasn't sure whether he regretted it. The carriage had been close, but it veered off towards Snow Hill. It was steep around here and Jude didn't recognise the area at all, but then the carriage went through some smaller streets towards what now appeared to be the outskirts of London and slowly he started to identify landmarks.

'It's not far, I recognise this area,' he said; the anticipation of getting back to where they had started was now acute. Susie felt the same, although part of her was reluctant to leave. She knew she would miss the vibrant atmosphere of the streets. She had come to realise that the people she had met were no different to the people at home. Except for their nature; they appeared to throw caution to the wind, no doubt due to their precarious and unpredictable circumstances. She looked over at Calvin. His normally upturned mouth, ready to smile at the drop of a hat, was latent now. He looked distinctly upset and she felt sorry for him. Jude was leaning forward and concentrating hard; they saw a few cranes and passed some rows of half-finished buildings and then eventually he recognised the lane with the three small houses; Eva's being the one on the far end.

'There it is!' he yelled. A little startled, Calvin asked the driver to stop and they all disembarked. Both Jude and Susie recognised the little vegetable garden at the front of the house, but there was no one around as it was still early morning. Calvin came towards them to say goodbye.

'You've been a great friend,' said Jude, 'we will always be grateful.' Calvin tilted his hat to them and gave a faint smile, he felt sad to lose them and wanted them to at least leave him an address, but he sensed it was futile.

'I will be keeping my eye on the news,' he said after consideration. He watched them wander off down the road which soon turned into a dirt track but didn't linger once they had disappeared from view. On reflection he assumed they were excellent at storytelling, yet in a strange way he knew he would miss their company, they carried with them a certain confidence that could not be explained. He got back in the carriage and took the long ride home.

Jude and Susie felt that they still weren't out of danger – they just hoped they would know where to go when the time came. A coach passed them, churning up dust and they stayed close to the hedge with their heads down. As they turned the corner Jude saw the windmill first and his steps quickened. Susie was at his heels and they both simultaneously broke into a jog scanning the hedgerow for a partition or something to show them the way they had come. Seeing nothing Susie panicked.

'We couldn't find the spot before, what makes you think we'll find it now?' But Jude had stopped and was looking further ahead.

'Come on, I think we are looking in the wrong place – we came through further back, I'm sure, nearer the windmill.' He began to speed up again. He wouldn't allow himself to believe that they couldn't get back. And then he saw it, the piece of her skirt that had been ripped off. It had moved from the road and was entangled high up in the bush nearby. He turned to Susie who was a few paces behind him. Suddenly he could feel that same pull that had brought them here.

'Quick!' he shouted and held out his hand. Susie grabbed his fingers but all he could feel was a swirling sensation in a vast emptiness. Moments later he found himself sitting next to the hedge in a setting that he was accustomed to. His head ached and he wasn't holding Susie's fingers anymore. He swung round to see if she was next to him. She was. The sense of relief was palpable. They sat leaning against each other for a while, as if to confirm that they had both been through the same experience. Then they felt a few spots of rain and got up off the ground. Everything around them was familiar – a handful of people were going into the main college entrance.

'Must be open then,' muttered Jude, not sure whether he was happy or sad. Susie could tell from the flatness in his voice that he had mixed feelings. They had escaped from a world that was vivid, colourful and alive. They had returned to a world that appeared to be asleep, a world driven by technology. They needed to see someone they knew and they eagerly went into the foyer. They stopped in their tracks. Written on the wall was the day of the week and time.

'That's unbelievable,' exclaimed Susie – it's the same day that we left, in fact, we've only been gone for half an hour!' They both pelted up the stairs towards the room they had left not so long ago.

'And here we are – it's as if we've never been away,' concluded Jude. There was a stunned silence in the room. Davy tried to gain some semblance of normality although his thoughts were well and truly scattered. He had so many questions. He decided to close the session early and tried to address the students in a relaxed manner.

'Well, that's it for today, I'm going to take Jude and Susie to the canteen to talk it over a bit more and I'll see you all tomorrow afternoon.' The class filed out one by one, all noticing the indescribable stench of manure and cologne. They could be heard in the corridor trying to find an explanation.

'Did you see the fire in their eyes?'

'Perhaps Davy put them up to it to get a reaction – well it certainly worked if he did!' Davy had overheard them and didn't blame them for thinking that; in fact he thought it was a good idea, a great way to bring history to life. He was thoughtful.

'Everything you said, the detail, the people, it was astonishing – but how is it possible? It doesn't make any sense – you can't travel back in time…and yet,' he pointed to Jude's chin, 'that stubble on your face, it wasn't there half an hour ago.'

'Well, it was all true,' said Jude. There was nothing more to say and he was exhausted.

'Come on, I'll take you home,' replied Davy.

As they walked to the car park Susie slipped her hand into Jude's. He squeezed it tight. Davy asked them to point out exactly where in the hedge they had emerged from. Recognising this must be a small sign of acknowledgement Susie showed him. 'Over there, where the two horses are standing, right at the far perimeter of the field.' Davy made a mental note of the spot.

As they dropped Susie off she looked troubled and Jude felt he could not bear to be parted from her. 'I'll come by tomorrow…as soon as I can,' he said. She smiled with relief and nodded as they drove away. Davy remained quiet. It wasn't too far to Jude's house. Jude knew what Davy must be thinking. He loved that era as much, if not more so, than Susie and somehow he knew that he believed them. He got out of the car and thanked him for the ride. He began to walk away but then returned to the car, tapped on the window and waited for Davy to wind it down.

'By the way if you're thinking what I think you are, can I give you one piece of advice? Take a hat.' Davy just smiled and drove off.